TO HAVE AND TO HOLD

THE VOWS BOOK 1

HEIDI RENEE MASON

BOOKS

Always Hope
Love At First Crepe (Sweet Escape 1)
Just Double the Recipe (Sweet Escape 2)
To Have and To Hold (The Vows 1)
For Better or For Worse (The Vows 2)
'Til Death Do Us Part (The Vows 3)
Nothing Hidden Ever Stays (Writing as H.R. Mason)

For information, contact the publisher, Hot Tree Publishing.

www.hottreepublishing.com

Editing: Hot Tree Editing

Cover Designer: Soxsational Cover Design

Paperback: ISBN: 978-1-925853-74-2

DEDICATION

This book is dedicated to my three daughters and women everywhere. You are stronger than you know. Be your own hero.

PROLOGUE

Moving as quickly as a woman seven months pregnant is capable of moving, Emma McCoy headed to the front door of her house. The loud knocking had awakened her from her afternoon nap. Emma yawned, trying to appear awake. She didn't remember being this exhausted during her other pregnancies. This time she could barely stay awake during the day.

"I'll be right there!" Emma called toward the general direction of the front door.

Emma wondered who it could be. Her best friend, Sadie, never knocked, and her husband, Jacob, was out of town on business. Her parents wouldn't have bothered knocking, knowing she would be resting while the girls napped.

She opened the door and was startled to see two policemen. Fear immediately crept up inside of her chest and nearly stole her breath away. Her first thought was that something was wrong with her parents. She prayed the policemen were at the wrong address, but a feeling deep inside her gut said they were not.

"Can I help you?" Emma's heart raced inside of her chest. She willed herself to be calm.

"Mrs. McCoy," the male officer started, "can we come inside, please?"

"Of course." Emma led them through the dining room and into her living room. She offered them a seat, but refused to take one herself. As the officers gathered their thoughts, Emma paced the living room floor. "Someone please tell me what's going on."

"Mrs. McCoy, please sit down," the female officer said. "We need you to stay calm. You're pregnant. You can't get so worked up."

Emma sat awkwardly in the antique rocking chair that had been in her family for generations. Her parents had gifted it to her when she gave birth to her oldest daughter. Her mother told her it would be perfect for rocking her daughter to sleep, and she was right. Emma ran her hands across the aged wood, thinking absently of her children, who were upstairs napping. Her palms were damp and her heart was racing. She tried to slow her breathing, but it was no use. She felt the need to vomit.

"Someone please tell me what's wrong. I know something's wrong." Emma looked directly at the officers, demanding answers. "Is it my parents?"

"Mrs. McCoy, there's been an accident. Your husband's plane went down while it was descending into Canada. The authorities have searched, but there were no survivors." The female officer looked intently at Emma, gauging her reaction. "I am so sorry to bring you this news."

"What do you mean? There must be some mistake. Jacob wasn't even going to Canada. He's in California on business." Emma breathed a sigh of relief as she realized the officers were mistaken.

"Look, I know this is a shock, Mrs. McCoy, but it has

been confirmed. The passenger on the plane to Canada was your husband. We have copies of his plane ticket and his passport. He's on the airport video surveillance. He boarded the plane with another passenger, a woman named Veronica Smith. Do you know her?" Both officers looked at one another before shifting their gazes toward Emma.

"Veronica Smith is our neighbor. She told me she was going to Pennsylvania to visit her family. Why were Jacob and Veronica on the plane together?" Emma's hands began to shake. "I don't understand. Jacob was going to California, not Canada." A million questions filled her mind.

She sat completely still for a moment as she tried to wrap her brain around the information. The small, nagging voice had plagued her for the past year, but suddenly it was screaming. She was stupid for not listening sooner. She'd always been suspicious of Jacob and Veronica, but she convinced herself it was paranoia. Jacob told her she was emotional because of the pregnancy, so she pushed aside the suspicion in order to keep the peace in her marriage.

Every image she had ignored paraded through her mind. She remembered all the times when she accused her husband of being too friendly with their lovely neighbor. With every accusation, Jacob would become incensed with anger, and Emma would always back off in an effort to avoid a confrontation.

Unable to ignore them anymore, each of the images came crashing down on her. She saw Jacob helping the beautiful Veronica trim the hedge between the houses. She saw them laughing together over a shared joke. She thought of Jacob's insistence that he was "just being neighborly." She recalled how her husband had placed his hand on the small of Veronica's back in a way that was too familiar for Emma's comfort. It was all too much to take in. She'd been right all along, and now she was playing the part of the clueless wife.

The room began to spin. Emma felt faint. Jacob was having an affair with Veronica, and they were both dead. She was alone, with two little girls and another on the way.

Emma tried to stand, but her legs wouldn't support her. The officers caught Emma as her body gave way and she slipped into oblivion.

ONE

"MAMA, it's time to get up now. Your alarm is going off," six-year-old Rose whispered.

Emma's eyes flew open and she jumped out of bed, wondering how she'd slept through the alarm again. Luckily Rose had climbed into her bed sometime in the night. If she hadn't, it was hard to tell how long Emma would've slept.

"Thanks, Baby." Emma planted a quick yet loving kiss on Rose's head. "Run and wake Lily and Dahlia for me, please? Tell your sisters we have to get moving."

"Sure thing, Mama!" Rose sprinted down the hall, yelling loudly for her sisters to wake up.

Her voice was nearly as jarring as the alarm clock had been. Emma cringed as the sound explosion of her youngest daughter reverberated down the hall. That was sure to wake the neighborhood.

Knowing she didn't have much time to get ready, Emma headed to the bathroom and turned on the shower until a plume of steam began to form in the room. Shedding her pajamas, she stood under the hot water, hoping it would wash away the sleepiness she still felt. Ten minutes later, Emma slid her favorite faded jeans over her curvy body, finishing the look with a black T-shirt and tennis shoes.

Not one to focus on her looks, Emma lifted a quick thought of gratitude for her long wavy strawberry-blonde hair. Not only was it one of her best assets, but the fact that it was wash and wear would come in handy on a day when she was running late. After a quick coat of mascara, and a shot of concealer to cover the dark circles under her emerald eyes, she declared it good enough.

Heading into the kitchen, she dropped bagels into the toaster and poured three glasses of orange juice for the girls. Knowing she needed a caffeine infusion immediately, she fixed a steaming cup of coffee for herself, making sure to add a generous amount of creamer. Emma loved the kick of coffee, but not necessarily the taste. She firmly believed the bitterness of black coffee needed a little help in order to be palatable. Even as the first sip coated her throat, she was already thinking about her next cup once she arrived at work. With the way her morning started, she was going to need all the help she could get.

"Girls, fifteen minutes until the bus comes," Emma called. "Get down here and eat, please!"

The sound of scampering feet echoed down the wooden staircase. As her girls paraded into the kitchen, Emma took stock of their clothing choices. Rose was dressed in her usual eclectic wardrobe. She had on a ruffled skirt with a polka dot pattern, paired with flowered leggings and a striped shirt. Rose was a firm believer in patterns, and Emma grinned at her youngest daughter's free-spirited ways.

Eight-year-old Dahlia followed closely behind Rose, dressed in her "comfy clothes," as she called them. Dahlia lived in sweat pants and T-shirts. The loungewear suited her middle daughter's lighthearted personality. Dahlia had always been an easy child. She often found ways to be helpful, and she genuinely enjoyed making other people happy. She was a perpetual sunny spot in an otherwise hectic world.

"Where is Lily?" Emma asked Dahlia.

"She's still figuring out what she's going to wear. You know every day is a fashion show for Lily." Dahlia giggled and rolled her eyes at her mother.

A few minutes later, the girl sauntered down the stairs with the regal air of a queen. The oldest of Emma's daughters had been born a tiny adult. Lily's mother often worried that the preteen was missing out on her childhood by being so serious, although she rarely brought it up in order to keep the peace. Lily had a difficult time with her father's death, and as a result, she had grown up too quickly. Lily wasn't playful and carefree like her sisters. Instead, she was serious and contemplative. Emma thought her eldest child had more worries than a girl of ten should have.

"Good morning, Princess Lily," she said with a smile. "It is so good of you to join us."

"Good morning," Lily answered with a scowl. She wasn't a morning person, and she wasn't afraid to let everyone around her know it.

"Ten minutes until the bus gets here, so eat quickly," Emma instructed the girls.

Not liking to be rushed, they grumbled and complained, but Emma gave them "the look" and they began eating.

Once the girls were off to school, their perpetually exhausted mother was left to clean up the kitchen, which wasn't too much of a hardship since it was her favorite room in the house. Large and sunny with a huge bay window that showcased the antique kitchen table, it was a nearly perfect room. As was the case in most homes, Emma's kitchen was the heart and soul of everything.

While she wiped down the granite countertops, Emma thanked her lucky stars that she didn't have a long commute to work. The coffee shop she owned, Morning Glory, was conveniently located next door. The shop's manager, Jane, an extremely capable woman and friend, allowed Emma to have mornings at home with the girls.

"Okay, I have five minutes to myself," Emma sighed and took a seat at the kitchen table, sipping her coffee while she thought of all of the things she had to do.

Emma was already bone-weary and the day hadn't even really begun. Being a single mom was a full-time job in itself, not to mention running a business and taking care of a very large house. If she thought about it all too long, it was overwhelming, but she scolded herself for whining. In spite of the hardships she had endured, she knew she was lucky to have all of it. Her daughters were exhausting, but she couldn't even begin to imagine how she would have survived the last six years without them.

When Jacob died, Emma spent the first few weeks in shock. If it hadn't been for the girls, she might have just given up, but being a mother wasn't for quitters. She knew she needed to figure out what to do with the rest of her life. She had been a stay-at-home mom for all of her adulthood, so she had no job history. Jacob was the breadwinner, and Emma found out that he hadn't been at all wise with their money. He didn't even have a life insurance policy, which she found out only when she needed it the most.

Like a slap in the face, she came to the harsh realization that her family had no income. Jacob had handled all of the finances, and Emma was oblivious to money matters. It came as quite a shock to find out that they had absolutely no savings, and quite a lot of debt. She had to make some tough choices, and selling their family home had been one of them. It wasn't an easy decision to come by, but she had no way to continue making the payments on her own.

Just when things seemed to be the darkest, her parents had come to the rescue. Emma and her daughters moved into the large rambling Victorian house in which she had grown up. She loved her childhood home, and was more than happy to seek refuge there with her parents. They had truly saved the day, allowing the young widow time to give birth to Rose and figure out their futures. The foursome settled into a comfortable routine in her parents' home. There was more than enough room for everyone, and they were more than happy to stay. The broken family settled into their new normal.

Emma's parents helped her when she needed it, but didn't interfere with the young mother's parenting when she asked them not to. Her father, a property developer, made a very comfortable living. He insisted she stay home and care for the girls as long as she wanted, telling her that being the mother of three children was a full-time job.

Two years passed, and Emma's dad decided to sell the building he owned next door. For several months, she had been hatching a plan, and she presented the idea of opening a coffee shop. Always her biggest supporter, Emma's father thought the building would be the perfect place for her to start a business. Rose had just turned two years old, and Emma didn't know the first thing about being an entrepreneur, but she did know that she needed a source of income. Again, her faithful parents stepped in and helped her get the business up and running. Emma opened Morning Glory, her trendy little coffee shop, the following year.

Just when things seemed to be going perfectly, tragedy struck again. Emma's parents were killed in a head-on crash on their way home from dinner six months after Morning

Glory opened. Alone once again, Emma was paralyzed with grief, unable to see her way to the other side. But like the angels they were, her parents provided for their daughter even after their deaths. The family home, paid in full, was bequeathed to Emma. She had a home and a means to support her girls, all thanks to her parents.

Feeling completely alone, her world was once again upended. She had no idea how she could care for three small girls plus run a home and a business on her own. She had no choice, but the task ahead of her seemed daunting. Out of the blue, her lifelong best friend, Sadie Ross, came to the rescue. Sadie moved into the upstairs apartment attached to Emma's house. The two women synced their schedules, and Sadie stepped in to help with the girls.

Emma McCoy had experienced her share of tragedy, but she was also aware that she had unbelievably supportive people in her life. Instead of seeing the tragedies, she tried to focus on the blessings. She had lost so much, but she always wanted to be thankful for the things she still had. Some days were harder than others, and being a single mom was exhausting. Emma drained the last sip of coffee and hoped that day would not turn out to be one of them.

"Break time is over." Emma sighed, rinsed out her coffee cup, walked out the front door, and headed to Morning Glory.

TWO

"Good morning, Jane," Emma called as she walked into the coffee shop. "As usual, the place looks great. I don't know what I would do without you."

"You know I love this place," Jane answered happily.

"And I love you," Emma said as she gave Jane a quick hug.

"I love you too. That's why you keep me around!"

Emma did love Jane. The woman was extremely competent. She was a few years older than Emma and had never been married. She was just sassy enough to be intimidating, and her blue hair, tattoos, and combat boots belied the fact that she was a kind, softhearted woman on the inside. The two women had become great friends, and Emma felt entirely comfortable leaving the shop in Jane's hands when she needed a break.

Morning Glory was a hubbub of activity. It was hip, trendy, and best described as "shabby chic." The easy atmosphere attracted both young and old alike, and the customer base was loyal. Emma herself couldn't believe the success it had become. The fact that it was the hottest spot in town was quite impressive for a woman who had started out with no idea how to run a business! When in doubt, Emma had adhered to the policy of "fake it 'til you make it." Unbelievably, it had worked.

Emma sighed deeply, knowing her agenda for the day included one of the aspects of her job she liked the least—shop inventory. She told Jane where she was going, then headed back to the stock room to get lost in the world of numbers.

She was hard at work and the time flew by quickly. Glancing at the clock, she realized she had been counting stock in the back room for over an hour. Emma declared it was break time, and she headed back to the front of the coffee shop, noting all of the familiar faces. One of her favorite parts of the job was interacting with her customers.

Scanning the room, Emma spotted an unfamiliar face in the crowd. Her heart skipped a beat as she surveyed the stranger in the corner booth. She had no idea how she had missed seeing him earlier, as he wasn't the sort of man who could possibly be overlooked. He was tall, muscular, and had raven-black hair that curled over his ears and fell playfully over his forehead. He was bent over a table full of papers, nursing a cup of coffee. If Emma were interested in men, she would have definitely been interested in that one. But she wasn't interested. Not in the slightest.

Emma had sworn off relationships after Jacob died. The hurt and betrayal she felt when she discovered his unfaithfulness was almost more than she could bear. Truth be told, Emma's relationship with Jacob had been rocky from the start, but she believed he respected the boundaries of the vows they had made. Unfortunately Emma found out that those vows made little difference to Jacob. His betrayal convinced her that she was better off alone. She couldn't live through any more heartbreak.

The stranger stood from the table, and his movement brought her back to the present. As he approached the counter, Emma took note of the fact that he was even better-looking than she had originally thought.

"This coffee is great. Could I trouble you for a refill?" The man's blue eyes sparkled like the ocean on a sunny day. It would be a strong woman who could say no to him. But Emma was a strong woman.

"Of course," she responded politely.

"My name's Liam O'Reilly. I'm new in town," the man said. "Is this your shop?"

"Yes," she said without elaborating.

"Do you have a name?" Liam laughed, and it sounded like music.

"I'm Emma," she replied. "And I need to get back to work. This place doesn't run itself."

She turned sharply, looking away from his penetrating blue-eyed stare. Without a moment's hesitation, she headed to the back room, needing to put some distance between herself and the stranger. Liam just stood there, looking at Emma as she walked away. His face was a mixture of both pleasure and pain.

Emma knew a man like Liam was probably used to having women fall all over him. She also knew that if he expected that reaction from her, he had another think coming. She wasn't some starry-eyed teenager who was going to swoon over a pretty face. She wasn't so easily won over. As she stacked boxes in the back room, she wondered why the man had gotten under her skin so easily.

Back at his table, Liam ruffled through the papers in front of him. He noticed Emma the minute she had walked through the door. He remembered seeing her once before, six years ago, when the police went to her house to tell her about Jacob's death. He was the FBI agent investigating

Veronica and her ring of jewelry theft. He had been at the site of the plane crash, and he was the one who had identified the bodies of Jacob and Veronica.

He flew back to Jacob and Emma's hometown of Beckland, Ohio, with the intention of breaking the news to Emma himself. When he arrived at her house, he was sidetracked by a phone call. Instead, the two local policemen informed Emma of her husband's death.

He remembered that first glimpse as she had opened the front door. The sight of her, nervous, pregnant, and about to get the worst news of her life had stayed with him the past six years. He couldn't get the image out of his head. Seeing her in the coffee shop had brought it all back to him.

Jacob and Veronica's case had haunted him for years. He had been so close to cracking it. He knew they were headed into Canada, and he had been waiting for them. It was a stroke of monumental bad luck that their plane had crashed. Liam's frustration was just as real at that moment as it had been six years ago. Tracking down the stolen jewels had become his life's work.

He recently bought the house where Veronica Smith used to live, hoping to find some clue as to where she had stashed the jewels. More than anything, Liam wanted answers. He wanted to close the case that he couldn't seem to forget. He had come to Beckland, the place where it all began, in the hope of learning more about Jacob and Veronica's illegal activities.

He believed that if he got to know Emma, he might glean useful information about her deceased husband. He had one goal, and that was to make friends with Jacob McCoy's widow in order to get to the bottom of the case. He knew it wasn't going to be easy, but he was up to the task.

Given the reaction he had received, it obviously wasn't

going to happen immediately. He knew better than to over-stay his welcome. Gathering his belongings, Liam headed out the front door, telling himself that he would try again another day.

Several minutes later, Emma returned to the front of the shop and noticed Liam was gone. She breathed a sigh of relief that she wouldn't have to deal with him anymore, although she had no idea why she was compelled to be so rude to him.

About that time, Sadie sauntered into Morning Glory. She came in each day during her lunch break. A research librarian at the Beckland Public Library, she was tall and thin, and had waist-length honey-blonde hair that looked like spun gold. If she hadn't been so genuinely sweet, it would have been very easy to hate her. Growing up, Sadie had stolen the attention of every boy in town. She was drop-dead gorgeous, with a line of admirers a mile long because she was too nice to tell them they didn't stand a chance. Emma loved her fiercely, and her best friend had the kindest heart of anyone she had ever known.

Dressed in her usual vintage attire, Sadie created a striking picture as she walked across the coffee shop. Sadie dated, but she had never been serious with anyone. Her life completely revolved around Emma and her daughters. Sadie was more than a friend to Emma; the women were like sisters.

"Hey, Emmy." Sadie planted a kiss on Emma's head before going behind the counter and helping herself to coffee and a bagel. "You look tired. You need a break."

"I'm always tired. But you're right, as usual. I'll come and sit with you." Emma grabbed her own cup of coffee and joined Sadie at a booth.

Emma had no sooner sat down than Sadie began talking

about her day. She divulged that there was a new shipment of books that needed to be labeled and organized, the circulation desk was understaffed, and they were in the process of renovating the children's section of the library. She talked for ten minutes straight, seemingly without ever taking a breath, but Emma didn't mind. She liked listening to Sadie, who was a great storyteller and made even the mundane things seem exciting. Everything was an adventure with her. She had the kind of enthusiasm that was contagious.

"And I have some more news. There was this guy who came into the research room today. Let me tell you, he gave the word hot a whole new meaning. Tall and muscular, black hair, and the bluest eyes I've ever seen. He sure made my morning. Believe it or not, he was nice too. He's in town from Chicago, and he's doing research on Beckland. Apparently he just bought a house here. I told him I would help him out if he needs it," Sadie said, eyes twinkling. "Maybe I'll end up with his phone number and a date before it's over."

"Was his name Liam?" Emma tried to sound nonchalant.

Clearly Sadie was referring to the same Liam whom Emma had dismissed earlier. Beckland was a small town, and a new, gorgeous man moving in was not something that happened every day.

"Um, yes, and you know this how?"

"He came into the coffee shop this morning. He introduced himself. He was doing some sort of work at the booth over there. I was really rude to him," Emma explained.

"Why were you rude? You're never rude." Sadie was confused by her friend's admission. Emma generally went out of her way to be kind to everyone.

"Well, to be honest, I'm not really sure why. Something about him set me on edge. I can't explain it," Emma confessed. "But I owe him an apology. I don't know what came over me."

The women chatted for the remainder of Sadie's lunch break. Before she returned to work, they made plans to have a girls' night out. They hugged goodbye and Sadie departed. Emma returned to the back room to finish the inventory, and the rest of the afternoon flew by. Before she knew it, it was time to head home to meet the girls.

She arrived at her house just as the bus pulled up in front. Lily, Dahlia, and Rose burst through the front door. Backpacks and jackets were discarded in the middle of the floor just as they were every day. Hugs and kisses were passed around, and each daughter began vying for her mother's attention. It was the beautiful chaos Emma loved about that time of her day.

Knowing it wouldn't be long before the hunger complaints began, Emma headed into the kitchen to start dinner. The girls planted themselves around the large kitchen table to do homework. Emma jumped in and began the daily routine, helping Lily study for a geography test and reviewing Dahlia's spelling words. Sighing, Emma read the note that Rose's class project was due in two weeks. The single mother was stretched too thin; she wished there were more hours in the day.

Two hours later, the family was sitting down to a dinner of spaghetti and meatballs. Emma was beat. All she could think of was a hot shower and sleep. Unfortunately there was still the kitchen to clean, lunches to pack, two loads of laundry to wash and fold, and the nightly grind of getting everyone tucked into bed.

It was eleven o'clock when she finally collapsed into bed. It felt good to finally be still. She had been going nonstop since six o'clock that morning, and it would start over again all too soon. There were always so many things that needed to be done. Doing them all alone was harder than she ever imagined it would be. In moments like those, Emma wished she had someone to share the load.

The nights were the worst. She was always busy during the day, so it was easy to push her loneliness aside. But when the girls were all asleep and the house was quiet, the solitude crept in. It wasn't the way Emma had imagined her life. She had never set out to be a single mom. She and her husband were supposed to be doing it together.

But a lot of things about her marriage hadn't gone as planned, even before Jacob's untimely death. The couple rarely saw eye to eye, and the spark had been gone between them for a long time. In her heart of hearts, Emma wondered if the spark had ever been there at all. The one thing they had in common, though, was their daughters. That had kept them together when they both knew they would have been happier alone. The sad fact was that Jacob and Emma's entire marriage had been nothing but an obligation for them both.

Emma tried not to dwell on her past, and most of the time she was successful. She didn't regret her marriage because her daughters were the result of it. That was one thing she could never regret. In spite of her fierce love for her children, she had been disillusioned by the whole mess of it. As a result, she had vowed to never become involved with another man again. Loneliness was better than being hurt. She would never allow herself to be that vulnerable again.

For the most part, Emma was fine with her decision, but there were times when she missed the feeling of partnership. Sometimes at night, the loneliness nearly consumed her. Over the years she got used to sleeping with the television on just for the sound. She hated the quiet most of all; all of her fears and thoughts of failure bred within the silence.

It wasn't as if she had to be alone. There were plenty of offers for companionship since Jacob's death, but Emma refused to become involved. A part of her died inside on the day Jacob's infidelity was confirmed, and she decided no other man would ever get that close to her. That was a chance she was not willing to take.

Exhaustion overtook her thoughts and her eyelids grew heavy. Strangely, the last thought before she drifted off to sleep was of Liam and his penetrating sea-blue eyes.

THREE

THE NEXT MORNING WAS HECTIC, WHICH SEEMED TO BE THE
new normal. Emma headed to Morning Glory after the girls
left for school and jumped right into work, knowing she
needed to finish her inventory accounting. Not a natural
businesswoman, money matters held little interest to her, but
it went with the territory. Once she was entrenched in the
task, the time flew by, and before she knew it, Sadie had
arrived for lunch. The women settled into their usual table
and Sadie began talking.

"So, I spent the morning helping that guy, Liam. You
know, the one we were talking about yesterday." It didn't go
unnoticed that Sadie had a definite twinkle in her eye when
she mentioned the man. "Let me just say that most guys can
only dream of being that degree of beautiful."

Emma rolled her eyes while Sadie went on about Liam.
Something about her incessant chatter irked Emma. Usually
she found Sadie's banter about men to be entertaining,
because she lived vicariously through her best friend's love
life. But hearing Sadie talk about Liam seemed to be having a

different effect. She didn't like the fact that Sadie and Liam had hit it off so well.

Of course Emma wasn't surprised that Liam was interested in Sadie. All men were. She would have questioned his vision if he wasn't. It shouldn't bother her that Sadie and Liam spent the morning together. The man was a complete stranger to her. She had also been anything but kind to him the day they met. He clearly wasn't interested in Emma.

Sadie, who had been oblivious to Emma's inner thoughts, continued chattering. "Liam supposedly bought a house in town. I think he's a cop or something. He's staying at a hotel until his furniture arrives. I don't know where the house is. He's been kind of vague about the research, just asks questions about the town and I answer him. He seems a bit mysterious," she finished.

Emma pushed her jealousy aside. "Well if anyone can help him, it's you, Sadie. No one knows the history of Beckland like you do."

"Thank you, my dear." Sadie smiled. "Well, I'm off to work. Are we still on for pizza and bowling with the kiddos tonight?"

"Yes, I couldn't get out of it even if I tried. And believe me, I've tried. It's not that I don't want to go, but I've been exhausted lately. I can't disappoint the girls, though. They've been talking about it all week." Emma reminded herself that she would do anything for her daughters. "Come down around six and we'll drive there together."

The women hugged goodbye and headed back to their respective lives.

∽

SADIE CAME in the door at exactly six that evening. She was nothing if not prompt and looked like sheer perfection. In contrast, Emma was a hot mess. The tired mother was daydreaming about a spa day as she tried to persuade her daughters to put their shoes on.

"Aunt Sadie!" all three girls squealed in unison as they jumped into Sadie's open arms.

Emma watched as her girls and her best friend embraced. Sadie was truly a part of their little family. The fact that they weren't blood relatives didn't matter. They were connected, and Emma was grateful every day for the support.

The group headed outside, climbed into Emma's blue SUV, and drove across town to Sam's Bowling, which had been a part of Beckland for as long as anyone could remember. Emma had spent many Friday nights there as a teenager, bowling with her friends. The place smelled like pizza, beer, and sweaty feet, but she had always loved it. It was full of memories.

They chose their lane, put on their bowling shoes, and placed their pizza order. They were fully immersed in the game when Emma glanced across the room and saw him. Her heart skipped a beat, and her breath caught in her throat. The heat rose in her body and her face flushed.

She didn't cover her reaction well, her gasp loud enough for Sadie to notice. Following Emma's stare, Sadie also spotted Liam. Emma had never reacted toward another man in quite that way before. She certainly hadn't reacted that way to Jacob.

"You okay, Em?" asked Sadie.

"Um, yeah, sure. I think it's your turn." Emma hoped her friend would be kind enough not to comment on her strange reaction to Liam's arrival. She also prayed that Liam wouldn't spot them and come over to chat. Unfortunately, heaven was not on her side, because Liam saw them and made a beeline toward their lane.

"Sadie, hello. I thought that was you." Liam gave Sadie a

quick hug. "Thanks so much for your help today. I really feel like I learned something about Beckland. I figure since I'm going to be living here, I should know as much as I can about the town."

"It was my pleasure," Sadie answered with a grin.

The two conversed easily for a couple of minutes. Emma observed them from afar, trying to push down the twinge of jealousy that reared its ugly head. The two obviously had hit it off quite well. They looked like old friends.

Emma knew she didn't have any claims on the man. Besides, she certainly couldn't compete with Sadie in the looks department. She was keenly aware that no man would ever choose her over Sadie. Not that she wanted them to. She wanted nothing to do with Liam or any other man.

"It's Emma, right?" Liam turned away from Sadie and offered his outstretched hand. "We met in your coffee shop."

"Good memory. Yes, it's Emma," she responded, reluctantly shaking Liam's hand.

As Liam and Emma shook hands, something unexplainable happened—it felt like a bolt of lightning shot straight out of Liam and arced into Emma. She had never experienced anything like that in her life. Shocked, she flinched and dropped Liam's hand like it was a piece of hot coal. Surprise and confusion covered his face, and hers turned an even brighter shade of red, though she didn't know if the flushing was a result of embarrassment or the consuming heat radiating inside of her.

Emma had no idea what to make of Liam. When he looked at her, she felt naked. It was almost as if he was able to see directly into her soul. It was disturbing and unsettling. She didn't like the vulnerable feeling she had with him. One thing she knew for sure was that Liam had also felt the jolt. His eyes widened and his jaw dropped so low it nearly hit the floor. Not knowing what to do, she turned away.

Sadie watched the scene unfolding in front of her. She had known Emma her whole life. She knew her best friend's every quirk, and she could tell immediately that sparks were flying between her and the new man in town. The chemistry between them was tangible. Sadie looked as if she might say something, but decided to keep her mouth shut.

Emma wished someone would rescue her before she made an even bigger idiot of herself. She was thoroughly flustered by the encounter with Liam. She couldn't bring herself to look at him. How could a handshake be so intimate?

Wanting to distance herself from the situation, Emma tried to appear busy by searching for something in her purse. About that time, her daughters noticed there was a new face in their little group.

"Aunt Sadie, who's he?" Dahlia inquired.

"Yeah, Aunt Sadie, is this another new boyfriend?" Rose giggled.

Lily just stood off to the side observing the situation.

"No, this isn't my boyfriend. His name is Liam O'Reilly, and he's new in town. He's been doing some research over at the library. I think he knows your mom, too, from the looks of things," Sadie said with a grin.

"He doesn't know our mom. If he knew our mom, we would know him." The suspicion and defensiveness in Lily's voice were barely contained.

Liam sensed right away that the older girl was protective of her mother. "You're right. I actually don't know your mom very well. I only met her yesterday when I introduced myself in her coffee shop. It's nice to meet you girls."

Rose and Dahlia politely shook his hand, but Lily simply nodded her regal little head.

Emma perched on the bench, completely mute through the entire exchange. Something about Liam threw her off-balance. The only way to deal with him was to avoid him, but Liam didn't make that easy with his open personality and easy self-assuredness.

Baffled by the situation, Emma tried her best to make it through the rest of the game. When the pizza arrived, she didn't eat any. She had no idea how to swallow pizza over the lump in her throat, not to mention the fact that she was so flustered by Liam's proximity that she felt nauseous. Thankfully, it wasn't long before the game ended, the pizza was gone, and it was time to go home. Sadie and Liam chatted easily with one another before saying goodbye. Emma's irritation grew as she watched the two of them together.

"Sadie, we need to go. The girls are tired and so am I," she said tersely.

"Yeah, sure, Em." Sadie was suddenly aware of her friend's obvious agitation. "Liam, I'll probably see you at the library tomorrow." Sadie made her way toward the door.

"Emma, it was a pleasure talking with you again. Your daughters are beautiful, but that's no surprise with you as their mother." Liam's smile was dazzling.

Emma decided the man was nothing but a smooth operator, and he was used to making women turn to mush. That was not going to happen to her.

"Goodbye, Liam." She didn't even try to hide the rudeness in her voice as she ushered her daughters out of the building.

Emma was sure he hadn't expected that reaction. There was only one way to fix the problem, and it was to stay far away from that man. If she knew what was good for her, she would stick to her guns. Liam O'Reilly was dangerous.

Out in the parking lot, Emma loaded the girls into the SUV without a word. Even though she realized she had no other options if she wanted to keep her heart intact, she was embarrassed by how rude she had been to Liam. She normally didn't treat people that way.

Sadie watched Emma with a confused look on her face. She had noticed the fiery chemistry between her friend and Liam, and she wasn't going to let it rest. When the time was right, she was going to have a long chat with Emma about what was going on with her. Emma had been attracted to men before—she wasn't a nun—but Sadie had never seen anything like the heat that had arisen from a simple handshake between Emma and Liam.

The group rode home in silence. The girls were worn out from the busy day, and their mother couldn't wait to get them home and into bed. She needed some time to figure out what was going on inside of her head.

Together, Sadie and Emma wrangled the girls into their pajamas. Their teeth were brushed, and they were tucked into bed. Once the women were alone in the kitchen, Sadie decided it was time to jump into the conversation.

"Em, what was that about at the bowling alley? You were so rude to Liam. I've never seen you act like that, so don't even try to tell me you aren't attracted to him. I'm surprised the bowling alley didn't spontaneously combust from all of the sparks you two were igniting."

"I don't know what you're talking about." Emma couldn't believe that Sadie had hit the nail on the head so directly. "I am not interested in that man in the least."

Refusing to meet Sadie's gaze, Emma went to the sink and put some water into the teapot. She could feel her friend's eyes on her, watching the rigid way she held herself. Emma was a ball of stress, and she couldn't hide it from Sadie. She knew her far too well.

"Em, what I saw back there with you and Liam was undeniable. There's no way you can say you didn't feel it. It was obvious to me and anyone else who was watching. There is a serious spark there. Why don't you just admit it?"

"Fine," Emma said, exasperated that she was so transparent to Sadie. "There's something about him that I'm drawn to. I'm attracted to him, and that scares me. I don't have time for men."

"Look, hon, I know Jacob hurt you. The man was a lying jerk. I never liked him. But sooner or later, you've got to move past it. You don't want to end up alone." Sadie wrapped Emma in her arms.

"I'm not alone. I have the girls, and I have you. I don't need anyone else," Emma replied stubbornly.

"One of these days, your girls are going to grow up and have their own lives. And I sure hope I'm not going to be single forever. I love you, Em, but don't let Jacob steal anything else from you. He's not worth it," Sadie counseled.

"It's too hard. I don't trust anyone, and I don't think I ever will. I'm hopeless, Sadie." Emma felt desperate to make her friend understand.

"You're not hopeless, just tired. You need to get a warm shower and go to bed. You look awful."

"Thanks a lot," Emma laughed.

"What are best friends for?" Sadie countered.

Locking the door behind Sadie, Emma trudged upstairs to her room. She carried her pajamas into the bathroom, turned on the shower, and let the hot water wash over her weary body. No matter how badly she wanted it, the deluge couldn't wash away the knots inside her stomach. She knew she should let go of Jacob's hurt and betrayal, but she didn't know how. She had been angry at him for so many years.

In some ways, the anger helped mask the hurt. As long as she was mad, there was no room for the pain. It was all so confusing. Emma didn't have time for love, or relationships, or Liam O'Reilly and his stupid blue eyes. She wished he would just return to where he came from and let her get back to normal. Her life wasn't exciting, but it was predictable, and she knew how to handle that.

Liam was anything but predictable.

FOUR

Emma stood laughing and chatting with a couple of her regular customers the next morning. After much turmoil the previous night, she'd made up her mind to forget about Liam. She didn't want to get involved in a complicated situation for which she had no time. As long as she avoided him, she wouldn't have to deal with her developing feelings for the man.

Morning Glory's front door bell jingled, announcing a customer. Looking up from her conversation, Emma's heart flip-flopped when Liam walked through the door. He caused a reaction in her that was difficult to ignore. Liam flashed a smile at Emma and headed her way. She wiped her sweaty palms on her apron.

"Good morning. You're looking lovely this morning," Liam said. "I'd like a coffee, if you're not too busy."

Emma forced herself to answer politely. "Of course. I'll bring it over to you."

She poured his coffee with trembling hands, praying she wouldn't end up spilling it all over him. Taking a calming breath, she headed to Liam's table.

"Here you are." She placed the coffee on the table while she carefully avoided eye contact.

He looked at her for a few seconds, trying to gauge the situation and decide the best way to proceed. "Emma, I'm not sure how I've offended you, but I get the feeling that you're trying to avoid me."

Liam smiled, and Emma cautiously allowed herself to look at him directly.

"You haven't offended me at all." The lie fell easily from her tongue.

"I make a living at reading people, Emma, and I'm quite good at what I do. I know when someone is avoiding me." He spoke gently, and something about his voice made her feel guilty about her strange behavior.

"Look, I don't know what's been wrong with me lately. I'm just tired, I guess," Emma reluctantly replied.

"Well it's no wonder. I'm sure it's exhausting keeping up with all you have to do," Liam said kindly. "Maybe you can take a break and join me for some coffee?"

"Well, I'll have to ask the boss." She sighed and let her guard down for the first time.

Their exchange caused something inside of her to shift. She supposed she could at least be civil to the man. After all, he was new in town, and he had been nothing but kind. He'd never done anything to deserve her bad treatment. It wasn't his fault that she couldn't trust herself around men.

Emma rationalized that they could just be friends, although that argument wasn't very convincing. She knew spending even a minute with Liam could lead to dangerous ground. But she also knew she wanted to. As she stood there waging a war inside of her mind, Liam waited expectantly. Finally, Emma sat in the booth opposite Liam. Once she allowed herself to take a breath, the two chatted easily for the next fifteen minutes. She couldn't believe how quickly the time passed.

"Thanks for the break, Liam. I need to get back to work, though," she said with a smile. "It really was nice talking to you."

"You, too, Emma. I'm sure we'll bump into each other again soon."

Liam gathered his belongings and headed for the front door. As he pushed it open, something caused him to turn around and take one more look at her. A nagging feeling inside told him he was playing a game that could easily back-fire if he wasn't careful.

Emma watched him go, thinking how nice their conversation had been. He was easygoing and seemed genuinely kind. In spite of that, she couldn't make time with Liam a habit. That would be dangerous for her heart.

FIVE

After school, Emma and the girls made the unanimous decision that the afternoon was far too beautiful to be spent indoors. On a whim, they headed down the street to the park. Emma sat on the park bench and watched as the girls played ball. The spring afternoon was gorgeous, and there wasn't a cloud in the sky.

Emma loved Beckland, and she believed it was the perfect small town. It felt safe, and she was happy to be raising her girls in the comforting familiarity. She knew everyone and everyone knew her. She had grown up there and was pleased that her daughters would also. The feeling of security was something a large city just couldn't offer.

The trees were starting to bloom, there were flowers popping up everywhere, and a lingering freshness was in the air. Lily, Dahlia, and Rose were kicking a soccer ball back and forth, laughing and running. Their mother was pleased to see them playing, carefree as children should be.

Glancing around, Emma watched as a dad pushed his daughter on the swings. A part of her always grew a little sad when she saw other children with their fathers. She thought of her own father, who had been amazing; she couldn't imagine her childhood without him. It made her realize how much her girls were missing out on.

With a smile, Emma recalled the time her dad had taken her fishing. He'd wanted so badly for her to like it, but Emma couldn't get over the slimy worms and the smell of fish. In the end, she hadn't enjoyed it as much as he had hoped, but the time spent hanging out with him was a memory she would forever cherish. She lost herself in the daydream, forgetting everything around her for a few minutes.

The piercing sound of Dahlia's scream ripped her from her reverie. Jumping up, she located the girls just in time to see their ball rolling into the street. Her hand flew to her mouth as Rose sprinted after it. The little girl was oblivious to the car headed in her direction. Rose was too far away, and Emma knew there was no way she could get there in time.

Instinct took over and Emma screamed loudly for Rose to stop, but her youngest daughter was on a mission to get the ball. Emma began running as fast as she could toward Rose, all the time knowing she would never make it before disaster struck. Time seemed to stand still and the world moved in slow motion. She was living every parent's worst nightmare.

Finally Rose heard her mom screaming, and she looked up as the car was within inches of her. Her face registered panic, but instead of moving out of the way, she stood frozen in place. Suddenly, from out of nowhere, a large man jumped in front of the car. He grabbed Rose and moved her to safety just as the car skidded to a screeching halt.

Running for all she was worth, Emma reached Rose as she and the man collapsed onto the sidewalk. The terrified mother grabbed Rose from the arms of the rescuer and realized in that instant that it was Liam. She didn't know where he had come from, but she did know he had saved her daughter's life. If he hadn't been there at that exact second, the car would have hit Rose.

Emma clung to Rose like a drowning person holding on to a life raft. The only coherent thought she had was that she would never let her little girl out of her sight again. She had almost lost her, and that was unfathomable. She fell to pieces, sobbing and cradling her daughter on the sidewalk. Once the tears started, they wouldn't stop, and soon Rose and both of her sisters, who had joined them on the sidewalk, were crying too.

Liam collapsed on the ground next to the others. He cradled his head in his hands and breathed a sigh of relief that he had been in the right place at the right time.

Once she regained her composure, Emma knew she had to offer her thanks. "Liam, I don't even know what to say. You saved my daughter's life. I don't even have words right now."

"Is she okay?" he questioned. "I hope I didn't crush her when I grabbed her. Did I hurt her?"

"Hurt her? Liam, she would have been hit by that car if it weren't for you."

As she spoke, the tears started once again. Emma was generally not the weepy type, but the thought of losing her daughter was enough to send her over the edge. She pulled all three of her girls into her arms and whispered a prayer of thanks.

Liam saw Emma as having a difficult time holding it together, and he knew someone needed to take control of the situation. He suggested they all go back to her house, where they could take a closer look at Rose to be sure she was okay. He lifted Rose into his arms and carried her toward the house. Lily, Dahlia, and Emma followed. Since she wasn't in the right frame of mind to act accordingly, Emma was grateful Liam had taken the reins.

The group arrived at the house and Liam placed Rose on the couch in the living room. The little girl hadn't said a word since everything happened.

"Rose, honey, are you okay? Does anything hurt?" Emma prompted.

"No, Mama," Rose replied quietly as she lowered her head.

"Baby, what's wrong?"

The little girl burst into tears. "I'm sorry, Mama. I know I shouldn't have run into the street. You always tell me to pay attention, and I didn't. I just wanted to get the ball."

"Oh, Rose, sweetie, I'm not mad at you." Emma knelt down and wrapped the little girl in her embrace. "I was just so scared. Please don't do that to me ever again!"

"I won't, Mama." Rose turned her small face up to Liam. "Thank you for saving me."

"Sweetie, I'm just glad I was there and was able to get to you in time," Liam answered with a smile.

"Girls, why don't you go have some quiet time in your rooms, please," Emma gently instructed. "It's been an exhausting afternoon, and you still have homework to finish tonight."

Obediently all three girls headed upstairs to their rooms. They were obviously tired, as they never did homework without an argument.

"Liam, would you like some tea?" Emma suddenly felt awkward having him in her home.

"I would love some, actually." He nodded and followed her into the kitchen.

Emma went to the sink and ran some water in the teapot before placing it on the stove. Now that she was alone with the man she'd been trying to avoid, she wasn't at all certain what she should do. She was questioning the fact that she had invited him to stay for tea when she should have politely thanked him and sent him on his way. The situation was far outside of her comfort zone.

But Liam had saved her daughter's life. That thought alone kept racing through her head. She realized she had treated him badly nearly every single time they had spoken, and yet he had been right there the moment she needed him the most. Guilt gnawed at her, and she knew she needed to apologize for her behavior.

"Um, Liam, I really need to say something to you," she timidly began. "I'm really sorry for the way I've acted. I promise I'm really a nice person. I don't know why, but every time you're close to me, my guard goes up, and I end up being rude."

"Yeah, I've actually noticed that," Liam said with a laugh. "So how about we start over?"

"I'd like that," she replied. She couldn't believe he had been so agreeable.

Liam walked toward Emma and her palms began to sweat. She had no idea what he was doing, and her heart felt as if it would explode inside of her chest. He stopped and stood in front of her, a mere couple of inches away. Her head tipped up toward his. His blue eyes met hers and she was lost. Any thoughts that she might have had about keeping her distance were immediately swept away.

Slowly, Liam bent down and cupped her face, gently caressing her cheek with his thumb. Emma took a few ragged breaths as he just stood there and looked at her. Time stood still, and they were both lost in the moment. For a second, Emma thought he was going to kiss her, but he didn't.

The snippet of time was interrupted by the whistling of the teapot. Emma was so startled that she jumped. Laughing nervously, she broke away and headed to the stove. Her head was spinning. She had no idea what was happening inside of her. She was quickly losing the battle to stay strong and keep her distance. But maybe she didn't want to fight the feelings anymore.

Taking a deep breath, she placed Liam's tea in front of him.

"Thank you, Emma," he said. "Now what?"

"I'm not sure what you mean," she lied.

"Come on, Emma. There's something between us, and we both know it. There's no reason to deny it."

Emma cursed him under her breath. She didn't like the fact that he was more than able to read her mind. Her defenses didn't stand a chance. She contemplated trying to pretend that she didn't know what he was talking about. But then she decided that maybe she should listen to her heart for the first time in years and see where it led her.

"All right then. I won't deny it." Emma's cheeks flushed as she looked at Liam and revealed her honest feelings for the first time. "Maybe that's why I've been so rude. I think I've been trying to ignore it and hide from it, but it's not working. I keep coming back to it. It's been a long time since I've felt this way. Maybe I've never felt this way. And I'm just rambling on here, so help me out."

Liam laughed as he reached out and grabbed her hand. "You know, I have no idea what to do either. Maybe we should start by going on a date?"

"A date? I feel like I'm back in high school all of a sudden," Emma giggled. "But I would like to go on a date with you. Where would we go?"

"I know this great little coffee shop...." Liam laughed. "Seriously, though, I would like to take you somewhere really nice. What do you think about that Italian place on Russell Street?"

"Vinnie's? That's pretty fancy." Emma wasn't used to dressing up and going to posh restaurants.

"You deserve to be treated well. Will it work for me to pick you up tomorrow night at seven?" Liam asked.

"Well... I don't know. What about the girls? I need to ask Sadie if she can sit with them. A date... um... maybe I shouldn't...," Emma stammered as she realized what she'd agreed to do.

"Emma, I don't know Sadie all that well, but I'm sure she will be happy to watch the girls. I'll pick you up at seven o'clock. And don't worry. We're going to have a great time." Liam bent down and touched his lips lightly to Emma's. She was so caught off guard that she could do nothing but nod as he walked out the front door.

Once he was gone, she grabbed the counter in an effort to stop her brain from reeling. She couldn't believe she had agreed to a dinner date with Liam. After all, she was the woman who had sworn off men and dating years ago.

Without another thought, she picked up the phone and called Sadie.

SIX

FOR THE FIRST TIME IN WEEKS, EMMA WAS UP BEFORE HER alarm. Her first thought upon opening her eyes was that it was date night with Liam. It was such a foreign concept that she repeated it to herself a couple of times. She hadn't been on a date since high school, and she had no idea what she was going to wear.

First things first, she needed to get the kids off to school before she could even think about the date. She awakened her daughters and the day was set into motion. The rest of the morning and afternoon whizzed by in a blur.

It was difficult to focus on work. Her thoughts kept going back to what had happened with Liam the day before. She felt light-headed just thinking about being that close to him. The kiss had been unexpected, yet spectacular, and it had all happened so quickly that she hadn't had time to process it. One thing she did know, however, was that she was doing a terrible job of keeping her distance.

Finally her work was finished and she headed home. Sadie had been more than happy to watch the girls, and she was picking them up from school and taking them out for pizza. After that, they were spending the night with her. Emma realized she had no one to focus on but herself.

The house was empty, and she wasn't quite sure what to do. Emma couldn't remember the last time she'd been alone in her own home, but she decided to take the rare opportunity to pamper herself. Grabbing the novel she'd intended to read a long time ago, she headed upstairs to the bathroom. Opening the cupboard door, she grabbed the vanilla-scented bubble bath that hadn't been used in forever. Turning on the water in the claw-foot bathtub, she generously dumped it in.

Undressing, she stepped into the steamy water and lowered her body beneath the bubbles. Relaxation was a rare commodity for her, and she was going to take full advantage of the moment. She filled the tub until it reached her shoulders, grabbed the novel, and began reading. She lost herself in the book for the next forty-five minutes.

When the water was no longer hot, she quickly washed her hair, shaved her legs and grabbed a towel. Drying off, she caught a glimpse of herself in the mirror. For the first time in a long time, she took a good long look at the woman peering back. She rarely gave her body any thought, but at that moment, she inspected it closely. Her fair skin had a rosy glow to it, thanks to the hot bath. She wasn't tall, and she wasn't short. She didn't have the long legs she admired on other women. She was curvier than most, but she carried it well. Her ample chest and rounded hips boasted a few stretch marks from her pregnancies. Overall, Emma didn't think she looked too bad for a thirty-year-old woman. She wasn't a runway model, but she had always been comfortable in her own skin.

But as the thought of Liam O'Reilly seeing her naked entered her mind, she began to feel a little less confident about her looks. If she believed she was nervous before, she was even more so as that idea popped into her head. As she thought about spending time with Liam and where it might eventually lead, she panicked a bit. Then she talked herself off the proverbial ledge. It wasn't as if the two would hit it off so well that they ended the night in bed. That idea was utter nonsense. Emma wasn't the kind of woman who would do such a thing. She wasn't easily persuaded.

She took a few calming breaths and decided it was time to get ready for her date. She took extra care with her makeup and put a bit more effort into her hair than usual, styling her long wavy strawberry-blonde locks with care. When she was done, she took a moment to admire the result.

"Not too bad, Em," she said to herself. "You clean up pretty well."

Going into her closet, she retrieved the green dress from the back. It had been four years since she'd last worn it, and she was hoping it still fit. She'd splurged on the beautiful dress for a fancy girls' dinner with Sadie, and she'd only worn it that one night. It had been hanging in the closet collecting dust ever since. Nervously, Emma pulled the emerald green dress over her frame and sighed with relief as it hugged her curves perfectly.

Glancing at herself in the full-length mirror, Emma was startled at the transformation. It was her, only better.

Her thoughts were interrupted by the ringing of the doorbell, and she immediately began second-guessing her decision to go on a date. She had sworn off men, and she certainly couldn't go on a date with one who made her react the way Liam did. Maybe she should just go downstairs and politely tell him she had changed her mind.

"Snap out of it, Em," she scolded herself. "Don't be ridiculous. Just answer the door."

Taking a deep breath, she headed downstairs and opened the front door. Her breath caught as she saw him. If she'd thought Liam looked good before, it was nothing compared to how he looked at that moment. His charcoal-gray suit was perfectly tailored to his exquisite body. His black hair was still wet, and it curled playfully around his ears. His sea-blue eyes locked on hers and time stood still.

"Emma, you are stunning," Liam said quietly.

"Right back at ya." The words just slipped out, and she mentally kicked herself for not having a better response.

Liam took her hand in his and led her down the front steps to his car, a shiny black Mustang. He opened the car door and helped her in before walking around to the driver's side. The couple drove across town in companionable silence, arriving a few minutes later at Vinnie's.

Jumping out of the car, Liam came around to open Emma's door and help her out. As he took her hand in his, he didn't let go, and she didn't want him to. The hostess seated them at a window table, the white linen tablecloths and candlelight creating the perfect setting.

"Emma, I know I said it before, but you look truly beautiful. You took my breath away when you opened the front door," he said with a smile.

"Thank you, but I have to be honest. I almost didn't answer the door. I was so nervous," she admitted.

"Well I'm glad you did," he replied as he reached across the table for her hand.

When the server arrived, they ordered their meals and chatted with each other as they waited for their food to arrive. The conversation flowed easily, and the nervousness Emma felt earlier was completely gone.

"So, tell me about your life, Liam," Emma said. "I feel like we've gone about this a bit backward. I feel strangely close to you, but I realize I know virtually nothing about you."

"Well, there's not a lot to tell," Liam began. "I'm an FBI agent, which sounds more exciting than it actually is. I'm from Chicago, but since I just bought a house in Beckland, I suppose I'm an Ohioan now. I've never been married, and I don't have any kids. I haven't even dated much, because work always gets in the way. I've been pretty focused on my career until now. And no one has gotten my attention enough to distract me… until a few days ago. I'm distracted by you, and I would love to know more about you."

"More about me… well, you know about my life. I'm a widow who runs a coffee shop and has three daughters. There's nothing more to tell." Emma realized how boring her life must sound to someone like Liam. "I'm not very exciting."

"I beg to differ," Liam laughed. "I find you to be anything but boring. I also know there's more to you than work and kids. Tell me about when you were younger. How did you meet your husband?"

"Well, Jacob and I knew each other our whole lives. We were both born and raised in Beckland, and we went to school together. Jacob decided I was 'his' when we were in high school. He was handsome and popular, and I guess I just went along with it when he decided we were an item. I never even questioned it. We dated all through high school, he proposed, and I said yes. All I really wanted to do was get married and have kids, so it seemed like the thing to do. I thought I loved him at the time, but I had no idea what that really meant." Emma was suddenly self-conscious that she'd revealed too much. The last thing she wanted to do was bore Liam with the details of her mundane life.

"Tell me more. Were you and Jacob happy?"

"I wouldn't say we were happy, but we weren't unhappy. That probably doesn't even make any sense."

"It makes perfect sense. Go on," Liam coaxed.

"I got pregnant with Lily, then Dahlia, then Rose. It all happened so fast. I was happy to be a mom. I had everything I wanted in my girls, but things between Jacob and me were stagnant." Emma shook her head as the memories began to resurface.

"I'm sorry marriage wasn't what you hoped it would be."

"I figured out pretty quickly that we shouldn't have gotten married. But I'd made a commitment to him and my kids, and I was determined to stick it out. I suppose that sounds pretty noble, doesn't it? The truth is I was afraid to make a change." Emma shrugged as she revealed one of the toughest parts about her past.

"I think it does sound noble, Emma. There aren't enough couples who stay true to the commitment they make to be a family," Liam replied.

"Well, the problem was that only one of us stayed true to that commitment. When Jacob died, I found out he was having an affair with our neighbor. Apparently I was too stupid to see it. Or maybe I did see it, but I didn't want to admit it."

"Emma, there's nothing stupid about trusting someone."

"There were so many things I allowed myself to ignore. I didn't want to see them, because I was afraid of what I would have to do if I did. In some ways I was set free when Jacob died, as horrible as that sounds. I'm blindly loyal, and I would have stayed with him forever, even though I was unhappy," she finished.

Emma took a breath. She was startled at how much she'd revealed to Liam. It was so easy to talk to him. There was nothing forced or awkward about it at all. She felt like she could tell him anything and he would listen without judgment. That was a rare quality in a person, and Emma was starting to understand that there was more to Liam than a handsome face.

"Wow, I sort of vomited out my life at you, didn't I?" she laughed.

"I'm glad you feel comfortable with me, Emma. It seems like we've known each other for years. I'm normally guarded with people, especially women. I've seen a lot with my job, and I suppose it's made me cynical. But with you, I feel at home. That probably sounds ridiculous," Liam said quietly.

"No it doesn't, Liam. I feel the same way, and Lord knows I've tried not to."

Emma was grateful she wasn't the only one having uncomfortable feelings. It was like the world had been put into fast-forward mode, as if she and Liam had known each other for years.

The easy conversation continued throughout the remainder of dinner. They shared tiramisu for dessert, then had another glass of wine to top it off. On the drive back to her house, though, the nervousness began to set in. Dinner had been great, but she wasn't sure what came next. She wondered if she should invite Liam inside, but she didn't want to be presumptuous. She had no idea how to handle the end of the date scenario.

She had the house to herself, but maybe she shouldn't put herself in the position of being alone with Liam, not knowing where that might lead. After second-guessing each possible avenue, she decided not to overthink. For once, she was just going to follow her heart. It was new territory, but she was coming to realize that she didn't have all the answers.

The car stopped in front of Emma's house and Liam helped her out. They walked to the front porch and simultaneously paused outside of the front door. Emma could tell Liam was also unsure about the moment.

"Listen, I don't want to assume that you want me to come inside, but in case you were thinking of asking, the answer would be yes." Liam looked into her eyes, and instinct took over.

Instead of replying, she pulled Liam's face to her own and brushed her lips against his. What started out as a gentle kiss quickly turned to something else. A spark that had long been dormant was ignited inside of her, and she knew there was no turning back.

Their lips parted and Emma fumbled in her purse for the house keys. Once they were inside, she led him down the hallway to the living room. They both sat on the couch, and before the situation could begin to feel awkward, Liam leaned toward Emma and engulfed her in his arms. He kissed her with such passion that nothing else mattered.

She wholeheartedly returned his kiss, wrapping her arms around him. He tangled his fingers in her hair and she pulled him even closer. They were lost in each other, neither one having ever felt that intense passion and urgency.

Just as she began to lose touch with reality, the cynical, distrusting voice in her head began its warnings. She had no idea what she was doing, and if she continued, things were going to go too far. She wasn't ready for that, so she needed to stop before they passed the point of no return.

Pulling away from Liam, Emma stood and began pacing across the living room floor.

"Look, I'm sorry, but I don't think I can do this. I'm not the kind of woman who can give herself to a man for just one night. I thought maybe I could be reckless and spontaneous, but that's not me. I'm guarded and careful—too careful, probably. Nothing about this is casual for me. There's too much at stake," she rushed on in a hurried voice before she changed her mind.

"Emma, look at me." Liam approached and tilted her head so he could look into her eyes. "Who said anything about one night? Have I led you to believe that this is in any way casual for me?"

"Well… I… uh… I mean…," Emma stammered. She didn't seem able to form a coherent thought.

"The minute I saw you, I knew you were special, and I knew if I ever got the chance to be with you, it could never be for just one night," Liam explained.

"I don't know what to say. I am insanely attracted to you. I don't scare easily, but I've been terrified since the first time I laid eyes on you because I know I could lose myself. Maybe I already have." Emma admitted the truth that frightened her to her very core.

"Emma, I just want to be close to you, whatever that means. I would never push you to do anything you're not ready to do."

"That means a lot to me. But I also don't want you to leave." Emma had no idea what she wanted, but she wasn't ready to see him go.

"I have an idea. Why don't you go take off your makeup, change into your pajamas, and climb into bed next to me? I know you must be exhausted from your long day, and I promise nothing is going to happen between us tonight. We're going to wait until we're both ready. I'll be happy to just hold you for a while," Liam said with a smile.

"That sounds like a really good plan. You have a deal," she answered.

Emma was beginning to see that Liam was a genuinely good man. There weren't a lot of guys who, given the situation, would have reacted like that. After all, she had brought him inside, kissed him passionately, practically ripped his clothes off, and then brought things to a screeching halt as quickly as they'd begun. And yet he wasn't angry or frustrated. He didn't push for more. Emma understood a man like that was a rarity, and she should hang on to him.

She did as Liam suggested, and within a few minutes, they were lying next to one another in her bed. What might have been an uncomfortable situation had turned into one of the sweetest moments she'd ever experienced, and Emma couldn't remember the last time she'd felt so safe.

For the first time in years, she quickly drifted off into a sound sleep.

<h1 style="text-align:center">SEVEN</h1>

She opened her eyes at seven o'clock the next morning, and it took a moment to get her bearings and remember why she was being held tightly inside a set of very muscular arms. Moving gently so she wouldn't wake the man sleeping next to her, Emma scooted out of Liam's arms. She couldn't believe the way things had gone the previous night. True to his word, he hadn't pushed for more. He simply held her and made her feel secure for the first time in ages.

She propped herself up and marveled at the sight of him, comfortably resting in her bed. He was truly magnificent to look at. He'd stripped down to just his boxer shorts to sleep, and looking at his muscular, chiseled body, she wondered how she'd resisted doing more than just sleeping.

She decided she would make him breakfast in bed, so she tiptoed downstairs to the kitchen to prepare scrambled eggs, bacon, and toast. After starting the coffee brewing, she set to work.

She was so engrossed in meal preparation that she didn't hear Liam enter the kitchen. As she pivoted from the stove to wash her hands at the sink, she jumped as she saw him sitting on the bar stool at the counter.

"How long have you been sitting there?" she asked as she caught her breath.

"Long enough to know I enjoyed the view," Liam laughed. "Good morning."

"Good morning." Emma suddenly felt shy. "Um, I was thinking we could have some breakfast? I hope you like bacon and eggs."

"Are there people who don't like bacon and eggs?" he asked with a grin.

"I don't know any."

She stood there a moment, feeling a bit out of her element. She wasn't used to preparing breakfast while a half-naked man sat at the kitchen counter. Swallowing hard, she took in the form of Liam sitting in her kitchen in nothing but his boxer shorts. It was a bit unnerving, which made it difficult for her to concentrate. Luckily the food was already finished, so she didn't have to think too hard.

"I hope you're hungry," she said.

She dished up two plates, putting a generous amount on Liam's. She poured him a cup of coffee and sat at the counter next to him.

"Thanks for breakfast," Liam said as he leaned in close to her.

He cupped her face and kissed her gently. The room was spinning, and fireworks were going off inside her body. It felt like a bowl of Jell-O mixed with a Fourth of July show. It was a good thing she was sitting down, because Emma was certain her legs would not have been able to hold her. She couldn't remember ever being kissed that way in her life. Jacob certainly hadn't caused that kind of reaction. She felt like she was truly alive for the first time. It was both scary and exhilarating.

All too soon, Liam drew his face away from hers. He grinned and began devouring the breakfast she'd prepared. Emma was too worked up to eat, so she just picked at her food. In the light of day, she felt a little bit unsure about what had happened the night before. Liam seemed fine about the way things had transpired, but she wanted to be certain.

"Listen, Liam, I want to apologize again for last night. I didn't mean to lead you on and then shift gears. I'm just really confused about what I'm feeling."

"Please don't apologize to me. There's no reason."

"I just want to try to explain. I'm afraid of getting involved. I'm afraid of trusting someone. I'm afraid of being vulnerable. I'm afraid of my girls getting attached to someone who isn't in it for the long haul. I guess I'm just afraid in general. I'm sort of a mess," she finished with a shrug.

"Look, I told you last night that I'm not going anywhere. We can take things as slowly as you need to. I know you've been hurt, but I'll do my best to earn your trust. You can count on me." Liam smiled.

The pair finished breakfast together, conversing easily about their pasts. Emma confided in Liam about the loss of her parents, and they both talked about their awkward teenage years, although Emma had a hard time imagining that Liam was ever awkward, sure he was exaggerating. She was struck once again by how easily the conversation flowed between them. There was nothing forced about it.

They finished eating, carried their plates to the kitchen sink, rinsed them, and loaded them into the dishwasher. Once again, Liam pulled her toward him and wrapped his arms around her. He ran his fingers through her hair, causing goose bumps on every inch of her skin. She wanted so badly to give herself to him, but she knew it was too soon.

She had to listen to that gut instinct that was telling her to take things slowly.

"Well, I guess I'd better get going. I had a really great time last night, and this morning. Thanks for spending time with me," Liam said.

"Thanks for understanding and being patient with me. You'll get tired of me eventually, but I just want to say that no matter what happens, you're a really great guy. You're a true gentleman." Emma was glad she'd allowed herself the opportunity to get to know him better.

"I'm a very patient man, Emma, and I guarantee that I am not going to get tired of you." He brushed her lips lightly with his.

After he left, Emma got ready for work. It was going to be a busy day at Morning Glory, but that didn't matter. She felt as if she were floating on air.

EIGHT

Liam headed to the library. He didn't have any research to do, but he wanted to talk to Sadie. He needed all the help he could get with Emma, so he decided to go right to the person who knew her the best.

Walking into the research room, he saw Sadie helping a library patron. She immediately noticed Liam and headed over to him.

"Hey there, how was the big date?" She grinned. "I haven't talked to Em yet, so I'll get the scoop from you first."

"It was great. Emma is really easy to talk to. She's funny and caring and genuine. And she doubts herself a lot. She also makes a killer breakfast," Liam hinted with a mischievous grin.

"You were still there at breakfast? Does that mean… never mind, Emma will tell me later."

"Well, I'm a gentleman, so I won't go into details. But we talked a lot," Liam said. "And the bacon and eggs she made me were delicious."

"Huh, what do you know? I think you've gotten to her," Sadie said in amazement. "If Emma let you spend more than a couple of hours with her, then she's starting to trust you. That's something I never thought I would see."

"I want her to trust me, Sadie. I know everything is moving fast, but I already have feelings for her. I need to make her see that I'm not going to hurt her."

"Want my advice? You need to take it slowly. Otherwise you'll spook her. Emma is terrified of getting hurt again, but she's even more afraid of her girls getting hurt."

"I would never hurt them," Liam insisted.

"You know, I actually believe you wouldn't."

The two chatted for several more minutes. By the time he left, Sadie was confident that her friend was in good hands with Liam. She couldn't wait to see how it was all going to play out.

AFTER LEAVING THE LIBRARY, Liam decided he wanted to see Emma again, so he headed to Morning Glory. He noticed she was hard at work, talking and laughing with her customers. As he watched her, a war of emotions began inside of him. He was indeed in a sticky situation, and he knew he had to proceed with caution. If Emma knew why he'd come to Beckland, she would never trust him again.

At first, all he'd wanted was to become friends with her in order to learn more about Jacob and his connection to Veronica. After spending time with her, though, it had turned into so much more. Liam was already invested in Emma. It had only been a few hours since he'd seen her, but he couldn't stay away.

Emma was pouring coffee when she noticed him sitting at the booth. She smiled, grabbed the coffee pot, and filled his mug.

"Long time, no see," she teased with a grin. It had only been a few hours, but somehow she'd missed him.

"Yeah, I couldn't stay away. I know guys are supposed to be aloof and pretend they don't care, but I can't seem to pull that off with you," Liam laughed.

"Don't worry, I won't tell anyone because that would totally ruin your image. Besides, I like it. I don't have time for games," she replied with a shrug.

"I'm sure time is in short supply for you. Between your kids and running a business, I'm not sure how you handle it all."

"Well, I don't have a lot of choice in the matter. The girls need taking care of, and so does the shop. I just do it. I put one foot in front of the other every day and get things done. There's no magic to it."

"I think you're wrong, Emma. What you do every day is definitely magic. You take care of the shop, your friends, your home, and your daughters. But who takes care of you?" Liam's tone became very serious.

Caught off guard, Emma didn't know how to respond. She was amazed at the things he saw when he looked at her. He seemed to understand what made her tick. She wished on a daily basis that there was someone to care for her. When the weight became heavy and pushed down on her shoulders with no end in sight, she prayed for someone who would share the load. She tried to be everything to everyone, but it was hard. If she thought about it too much, she was over-whelmed.

"Well, Liam, I guess I take care of myself," she answered evenly.

NINE

AFTER FINISHING WORK AT MORNING GLORY, EMMA HEADED home. She was bone-weary, and the last thing she wanted to think about was the mountain of chores waiting for her. The bright yellow school bus rounded the corner at three thirty, just like clockwork, and all three girls came running to greet their mother. She listened while they all tried to talk to her at the same time, smiling as they told her about their day and all of the things that had happened.

Once they were inside, she told them to get homework started. With only a little bit of argument, they did as she said. While they worked, Emma went into the laundry room and started a load. There was always a giant pile, and if she missed a day, it multiplied exponentially.

While it washed, she helped Rose, who was struggling with a math problem. Once that was tackled, she went to the refrigerator to decide what to make for dinner. She was completely burned out, and the last thing she wanted to do was cook. As she peered inside waiting to be inspired, the doorbell rang.

Emma went to the front door and opened it. To her

surprise, a delivery man from Chen's Chinese Garden was standing there holding a box filled with food.

"Can I help you?" Emma had no idea why he was at her front door.

"Is this 3321 State Street?" the man inquired.

"Yes, it is, but there must be a mistake. I didn't order anything."

"Is your name Emma McCoy?"

"It is." She had no idea what was going on.

"Then this is for you. There's a note attached that might explain it." He placed the heavy box in her arms. "No need for a tip. It's already been taken care of."

"Thank you," she called to the man as he left.

Confused, she carried the box into the kitchen and placed it on the counter. Lying on top of the aromatic food was a note. Intrigued, she opened it.

"Emma, you seemed really tired today, and I wanted to make your night a little easier. I hope you and the girls like Chinese food. Yours, Liam"

She couldn't believe it. Liam had thought ahead, knowing how tired she'd been earlier. He had taken something off her to-do list just to make her night a bit easier. He was such a thoughtful man, and she'd never known anyone quite like him. He was making it difficult for her to take things slowly.

The girls came into the kitchen, and when they saw the box of Chinese food, they let out a loud cheer. She explained to them that Liam had sent it.

"Liam is really nice, Mom," Rose said.

"Yeah, I think you should go out on another date with him," Dahlia agreed.

"You're awfully quiet, Lily." Emma was uncertain how her oldest daughter felt about her mother dating. "What do you think of Liam?"

"He seems like a good man," Lily said quietly. "It's okay with me if you want to date him."

"It sounds like you're all on the same page, and that's important to me. You know we're a team. I won't do anything you aren't ready for. I'm not sure what's going on with me and Liam, but he's really thoughtful, and I like him a lot." As she said the words, she realized they were true. "I want to spend more time with him."

"Good for you, Mom," Lily replied.

"Let's eat Chinese food!" Rose squealed.

After dinner, Emma cleaned up the kitchen and tucked her daughters into bed. Then she took the laundry from the washer and put it into the dryer, all the while thinking of Liam. He was always in her thoughts these days.

After the laundry was done and the girls were asleep, she retreated to her room. She hopped into bed and grabbed her phone, debating whether she should call Liam or text him. Deciding that such a nice gesture deserved a phone call, she dialed his number. The phone rang only once before he picked up.

"Hey, Emma," said Liam.

The sound of his voice alone was enough to make her heart beat a little faster. It was hard to believe that he could have such an effect on her.

"Hey there," she responded. "I had to call you. What you did today was basically one of the most thoughtful things anyone has ever done for me."

"I'm glad I could help. You take care of everyone all the time. I just thought someone should take care of you for once."

"It was nice not to have to think about dinner for a change," she laughed. "That's my least favorite part of the day."

"So, what are you doing right now?"

"Well, I'm sitting in my bed talking to you."

"What are you wearing?"

"You don't even want to know." She giggled as she looked at her threadbare pajamas. "It's very unsexy."

"You could make anything look sexy, Emma," Liam replied.

Her heart was racing, and she knew she was hooked on the man.

"So when are we going out again?"

"Did you have something in mind?" She knew the answer was no longer *if* she would see him but *when*.

"I was thinking maybe I would take you and the girls out for dinner and an early movie on Thursday. What do you think?" Liam asked.

He was not only asking her out, but he was including her children as well. Emma's heart melted a little bit more. He had figured out that her daughters were her weakness, and he was playing his hand well.

"I would like that, and I'm guessing the girls would too. Do you like princess movies? Because I'm pretty sure I haven't watched a movie without a princess in it for ten years," she warned.

"Princesses happen to be my favorite," Liam laughed.

They chatted on, and before she knew it, an hour had passed.

"As much as I don't want to hang up, I need to get some sleep now," she said. "Thank you again for dinner."

"It was my pleasure," Liam replied. "And you'll probably see me at the shop tomorrow. It'll only be Wednesday, and I have this need to see you every day."

"Well, Thursday does seem awfully far away. See you soon, Liam."

TEN

Sitting in the darkness, the man watched and waited. Scoping out Emma's house was his new favorite pastime. She had the answers he needed. He had followed her for months and had learned her routine. He had watched her, observed her movements, waiting for the right time. His plan would be set into motion soon, and when it was, she would tell him everything.

Glancing toward the lovely Victorian house, he saw the upstairs lights go off. He knew she was probably falling asleep, feeling warm and safe in her bed.

"Enjoy your security while you can, Emma. Before long, everything changes."

The man started the car and drove off into the night.

ELEVEN

The buzzing of the alarm startled Emma the next morning. Taking a moment to stretch and fully awaken, she found that her first thoughts of the morning were centered on Liam. She recalled the wonderful dinner arrangements he had made the night before. He was surprising her at every turn, and was definitely not what she'd expected. He was concerned for her well-being, and he cared about her feelings.

Emma pondered her relationship with Jacob, and she realized Liam was made of completely different stock than her late husband. Jacob had only been interested in what she could do for him; he would have never thought of doing something nice for her unless he somehow benefitted as well. Being around Liam was a whole new experience, and she was quickly learning to enjoy it. But the fact that she felt so attached to him already was a bit scary.

Emma headed downstairs to begin the day. Stepping onto the front porch to grab the newspaper, she took in the signs of spring. Her mother had always had a green thumb, so the yard was beautifully landscaped. She did not inherit that particular talent, so she paid the neighbor boy to mow and do the trimming and weeding. He had a knack for keeping her mom's flowers alive, and the cheerful daffodils were already starting to bloom.

Inspired by the spring flowers, she ran into the kitchen, grabbed the scissors, and cut a bunch of them. Taking them inside, she filled her prettiest vase with water. Placing the daffodils on the table, she smiled at the brightness they brought into the kitchen. Humming to herself, she started the pancakes.

An hour later, she sent three very happy girls off to school with tummies full of pancakes. She finished cleaning the kitchen, then made a spur-of-the-moment decision that she was going to take the morning off. It had been quite some time since she'd done so, and Jane would be more than happy to cover the shop for the morning. Her trusted manager was always telling her to take more personal days, and for once, she was going to listen.

After she made plans for a few hours of alone time, she wondered what she was going to do with it. Deciding she wanted a new outfit for her date with Liam, she opted to walk to the local boutique. The day was perfect for a leisurely stroll, so she grabbed her purse and headed out the front door.

Très Chic, Beckland's nicest clothing store, was about five blocks away. As she strolled down the sidewalk, she realized she had no idea when she had last gone shopping for clothing. She always bought things for the girls, but she rarely spent money on herself. The prospect of a new outfit put an extra spring in her step.

She was almost to the boutique when the hairs on the back of her neck stood on end. She had the strangest sensation that she was being followed. Looking behind her, she noticed a green sedan ease into a parking spot along the street. A tall man, dressed completely in black, got out of the car and dropped some coins into the parking meter. He glanced around, seemingly trying to decide which direction to go.

Emma had no idea why she noticed the man, but something about him made her uneasy. He looked sinister. She had never seen him before, and in a small town like Beckland, strangers were unusual. It might all amount to nothing, but in spite of the warm morning, she shivered.

"Emma, you're just paranoid," she scolded herself. "Don't be ridiculous."

Laughing nervously, she pushed the nagging thought aside and walked into the trendy boutique to see what she could find.

"Hey, Emma," Nora, the owner of Très Chic, greeted. "I haven't seen you in a while. How have you been?"

"Hi, Nora. I'm great!" She looked around the shop at all of the lovely clothing. "The shop looks good. It's been so long since I've been here that I forgot."

"Are you after something special or just looking around?"

"Well, I'm not really sure what I'm looking for. I guess I was hoping you'd help me. I need a new outfit."

"Casual or dressy?" Nora asked.

"Well, casual, but kind of… well, sexy, I guess." The thought of coming across as "sexy" was so far out of her comfort zone that even saying the word was embarrassing.

"Well, with your curves, sweetie, you can definitely pull that off. Just leave it to me. You're such a knockout that you're going to make my job a piece of cake. Trust me."

"Okay, but go easy on me," she laughed.

Nora had a keen eye for fashion, and she was always

impeccably dressed. Emma told herself to calm down and trust the professional.

"I'll be back in a minute with some things for you to try." She led Emma to the dressing room and disappeared into the clothing racks.

Emma waited nervously. She wasn't used to having the focus on herself, and it made her uncomfortable.

"Here, sweetie, start with these." Nora handed her a pair of jeans and a shirt. "And don't say no until you've tried them on."

She looked at the clothing Nora had hand-picked. They were items Emma would have never chosen, but were much classier than her usual baggy jeans and T-shirts. She slid on the formfitting jeans and black low-cut blouse. Looking in the mirror, expecting the worst, she was shocked to find that she looked better than she imagined. The outfit was more daring than her usual attire, but she actually liked the way the garments hugged her curves. She was impressed with Nora's ability to pick out the perfect pieces on the first try.

"Nora, you're a genius," she called through the dressing room door. "I'll take the whole outfit. Can you recommend some shoes too?"

"I have the perfect pair of size eights waiting for you at the counter," Nora laughed, sounding quite pleased.

A few minutes later, the jeans, blouse, and flowered wedges Nora had picked out were stashed in the shopping bag. Happy with her purchases, Emma headed home. As she walked, she lost herself in a wonderful daydream about Liam, then realized she hadn't been paying attention to her surroundings.

Glancing around, she noticed the strange car from earlier was driving slowly behind her. Her instincts were on high alert, and she picked up her pace a bit. She wasn't sure if the car was following her or if it was all just a coincidence. Either way, it made her uneasy.

She arrived home and went inside. As she pushed the nagging thoughts aside, she failed to notice that the car lingered in front of her house long after she'd stopped thinking about it.

TWELVE

At six o'clock the next evening, Emma was putting the finishing touches on her appearance. The jeans and blouse looked amazing, and the flowered shoes added a touch of whimsy. She knew she looked good, and it gave her the confidence boost she needed.

The doorbell rang and she hurried downstairs. When she opened the front door, the sight of Liam quickened her pulse. He had dressed casually, in faded jeans and a polo shirt, but he was just as handsome as he'd been in his tailored suit.

"Hi there." Liam grinned as he presented Emma with a beautiful bouquet of wildflowers. "I brought you these."

"Thank you, Liam." She smiled as she inhaled their scent. "It looks like you still have something behind your back. What's the secret?"

"You'll see. Where are the girls?"

About that time, Lily, Dahlia, and Rose came running down the stairs.

"Hello, ladies," Liam greeted them.

"Hi, Liam," they answered in unison.

Rose ran forward and gave him a big hug. He had become her hero since the day he'd rescued her from the car.

"I have something for you, Rose," Liam said as he handed her a small stuffed dog. "I hope you like stuffed animals."

"I *love* them, Liam. How did you know dogs are my favorite?" Rose asked with wide eyes.

"Just a good guess," he laughed.

Dahlia and Lily weren't quite so exuberant, but they both smiled politely as they watched Liam and Rose.

"Don't worry, I didn't forget you two. Dahlia, I got you the new Cammy Cooper book. I hear it's what all the girls are reading, and it just came out today. I hope you like it." Liam handed the book to Dahlia and a smile covered her entire face.

"I've been waiting for this book! Mom said she would take me to the bookstore this weekend, but now I don't have to wait! Thank you, Liam." Dahlia beamed.

"Lily, I got you some flowers like your mom's. I figured a lady always likes flowers." Liam handed another bouquet of wildflowers to Lily.

"Wow, no one has ever bought me flowers before," she said shyly. "Thanks, Liam."

Lily and Emma headed into the kitchen to put their flowers into water. When they returned, Liam, Dahlia, and Rose were in a very serious conversation about the movie choice for the evening.

"So, girls, what movie are we seeing tonight? I thought we could go for pizza before the movie, too, if that's okay," Liam suggested.

"We're always hungry," Dahlia laughed.

"Mom said maybe we could see the new *Princess Mysteries* movie. I'll bet that doesn't sound fun to you, though," Lily said to Liam.

"Don't be so sure about that. I'll have you know that I've seen all of the *Princess Mysteries* movies. My niece is your age, and I always take her to see them." Liam laughed at the shock on Lily's face.

"I didn't expect you to know what they were," she answered.

"I'm full of surprises," he replied.

Everyone piled into the SUV and drove to Pete's Pizza. They gorged themselves on pizza until Emma was sure the girls were going to burst. After that, the group headed to City Center Cinema. Liam purchased the tickets for the show, and they made their way into the darkened theater. Ninety fun-filled minutes later, the movie was over and they were on their way home, singing the theme song for the *Princess Mysteries.*

Emma couldn't believe how wonderfully the night had gone. Liam was funny and interesting, and the girls had taken to him right away. Rose had even grabbed his hand as they walked to the car. Her daughters were cautious of strangers, especially men, but everything was different with Liam. It all felt so easy, almost as if they'd been together for years. Emma knew they were all smitten by him.

Arriving at her house, they all headed inside. She instructed the girls to go straight upstairs and get into their pajamas, get their teeth brushed, and be ready for their tuck-in. Liam stood awkwardly by the front door, and Emma knew he was unsure of whether or not he should come in.

"Liam, make yourself comfortable. I'll get the girls into bed and we can have some tea."

"Okay. Can I help you with anything?"

"No, I've got the bedtime routine down," she laughed as she directed him to the living room.

Liam settled himself on the couch and Emma headed upstairs. It wasn't long before she returned.

"Um, Liam, the girls would like for you to come upstairs and tell them good night. But if that's weird or anything, you totally don't have to." Emma wasn't sure how he would respond.

"Of course. I wanted to, but I didn't want to overstep," he answered.

He stopped in the doorway of each girl's room to say good night, and Emma smiled. Her girls liked him so much already, and so did she.

Liam couldn't believe what an amazing job Emma had done in raising those girls alone. They were polite and well-mannered, and they had quickly won his affection.

The pair went into the kitchen, and Emma put the tea kettle on the stove. Settling himself at the counter, Liam watched.

"You have amazing girls. You must be very proud," he said.

"I am. They're wonderful. I don't know what I would do without them. They seem quite taken with you," she replied.

"Well, the feeling's mutual." He walked across the kitchen to where she was standing. "I'm also quite taken with their mother."

He leaned down and kissed her, and the response was immediate and heated. Wrapping her arms around his neck, she melted into him. She had serious feelings for Liam. He had broken down her walls one brick at a time. She loved the way he made her feel, but watching how great he was with her daughters convinced her that she was ready to give their relationship a chance.

She pulled Liam's face toward hers, and their mouths met with intense fire. There was no way she could extinguish the flame, and she didn't want to.

Emma had tried to keep her distance with Liam, not to let

him in. Despite her best efforts, he had gotten beneath her skin and had broken down the barriers. She felt awake with Liam, and more alive than she ever had before. After years of merely existing, she was finally living.

With Liam, she was complete.

THIRTEEN

Emma awakened the next morning to find her limbs entwined with Liam's. She blushed a little, thinking of the night before. It had been wonderful, and she didn't regret a thing. Sometimes decisions made in the heat of the night were regretted in the light of day, but she didn't feel that way at all. She was convinced that what they had was a good thing.

"Morning," Liam said sleepily as he snuggled closer.

"Morning. You're welcome to stay here, but any minute, I'm going to have three girls knocking on the door wondering why it's locked, so I need to get up." She was a little bit nervous about how to handle things with her daughters.

"Do you mind if I take a quick shower?" he asked.

"Sure, make yourself at home. There are clean towels in the cupboard. I'm going to make some coffee and breakfast."

Emma went downstairs and grabbed the ingredients for waffles. She didn't know how she was going to explain Liam's presence, but she would figure that out when the moment came. She was "flying by the seat of her pants" and had no clue how it would all play out.

She finished the waffles and called the girls downstairs. They were excited to see their favorite breakfast.

"These are yummy, Mama," Rose said with her mouth full.

"Thanks, sweetie, but please finish chewing before you talk." She gave Rose a kiss on the top of her head.

They finished eating, took their plates to the sink, and headed upstairs for their backpacks. She glanced at the stairs, wondering where Liam was. A couple of minutes later, the girls ran downstairs, backpacks in place, ready for school. She walked them to the curb just as the bus came around the corner. Kissing them goodbye, she went back inside and found Liam in the kitchen, helping himself to a plate of waffles.

"There you are. I thought maybe you got lost in the shower," she said.

"Well, I just waited upstairs until I heard the girls leave. I didn't know if you were ready to explain the fact that I was here."

"That was really thoughtful of you. Thank you for being so considerate of their feelings," she replied as she planted a kiss on Liam's mouth.

"You know, I could definitely get used to this. It doesn't get better than eating homemade waffles and kissing a beautiful woman first thing in the morning."

"Well I aim to please, Mr. O'Reilly." Emma felt practically giddy with delight.

"Since you made breakfast, I'll clean the kitchen while you shower and get ready for work," Liam said kindly.

"You have a deal." She kissed Liam quickly before heading upstairs.

Liam set to work cleaning the countertops and stove, then loading the dishwasher. He couldn't believe what an amazing woman Emma was. They fit together so well. He could definitely see a future with her, and the girls were an added bonus. He'd always wanted a family, but he'd never found the right woman before.

He was convinced that Emma was the one for him, and he was pretty sure she felt the same way. But knowing her past, he wasn't going to push things with her. He would be patient and let her set the pace.

The nagging thought in the back of his mind was his connection to Jacob. If Emma found out before he told her himself, all of the progress they'd made would be ruined.

He knew he should tell Emma that he was the FBI agent investigating Jacob and Veronica. But that could go very badly for him, and a part of him thought he should keep it hidden and hope it stayed that way. Neither option sat well with him. If he told her, she might panic and think he'd been trying to get close to her to find out more about Jacob. Granted, that had been the case in the beginning, but that all changed once he got to know her.

The closer he'd gotten to Emma, the less Jacob mattered. He was in love with her, but if she discovered that his original reason for coming to Beckland was her late husband, she would never believe his feelings were genuine.

The best resolution was the path of least resistance. He decided not to tell Emma about his connection. The odds of her finding out on her own were slim, and he didn't want to risk their budding relationship. He wouldn't tell Emma, and he prayed she never found out on her own.

FOURTEEN

Things moved along well over the next couple of months, and Liam and Emma were inseparable. He joined them each night for dinner. He always stayed over, but he made sure he was gone in the morning before the girls woke up. They weren't trying to be secretive, but Emma wanted to be sure they were headed toward a future together before telling her daughters about the seriousness of the relationship. Lily, Dahlia, and Rose all loved Liam, and they'd grown accustomed to him being there. Emma trusted him more every day.

Liam was barbequing steaks for dinner, so they invited Sadie to join them after work. Emma enjoyed having a man around. The day before, her kitchen sink clogged. Normally she would have picked up the phone and called a plumber, but Liam jumped in and fixed it. Although she wasn't used to being taken care of, she found that she liked it.

She was putting the finishing touches on the salad when Liam came up behind her and wrapped his arms around her waist.

"I didn't even hear you come in," she said as she gave him

a kiss.

"I snuck in when you weren't looking."

"Good thing you didn't surprise me too much, considering this sharp knife in my hand."

"How was your day?" Liam asked, settling himself at the kitchen counter.

"It was good. We were pretty busy at the coffee shop, which I'm not complaining about. It makes paying the bills a lot easier."

"My day was good, too. My furniture has been in storage, and I finally told them to deliver it. The truck arrived, so it looks like I get to start moving into my house. I'm not looking forward to unpacking."

"I'll help if you need it," she said. "You know, I haven't even seen your house yet. You always come here."

"Once I'm unpacked, we'll have dinner at my place." Liam was dreading the moment when Emma discovered he'd bought Veronica's old house.

"The steaks are already out," she said as she gestured across the room. "I marinated them all day, so they should be tasty."

Liam grabbed the meat and went into the backyard. A few minutes later, Sadie arrived. Emma handed her friend a glass of wine and told her to go and relax. After she finished up in the kitchen, Emma joined them. The girls were playing in the backyard, and Sadie, Liam, and Emma talked and cooked steaks on the grill. It was the perfect afternoon.

Emma couldn't believe her good luck. She would have never imagined herself at this point a few months ago. She didn't want to jump to conclusions, but she could envision her future with Liam. As a matter of fact, she had a hard time remembering how things had been without him. In the span of a couple of months, he had become an integral part of her life.

"So, Liam, Emma tells me you're ready to start moving into your house," Sadie said.

"Yeah, it seemed like it would never happen, but the house is ready, my furniture is here, and it looks like it's time," Liam replied.

The home phone rang inside the house, and Emma ran inside to answer it.

"Hello," she said.

No one replied, but she could hear breathing on the other end of the line.

"Hello? Is anyone there?" she repeated.

There was still no answer, but Emma knew she heard someone on the line.

"Hello? Is someone there?" she tried a third time.

The line went dead. Feeling slightly uneasy, Emma hung up the phone and went back outside. She was sure she'd heard someone breathing.

"That was weird. I guess it was a wrong number. Probably a telemarketer." She shrugged. "It looks like the steaks are done, huh?"

"Yep. Girls, it's dinnertime," Liam called out.

Lily, Rose, and Dahlia came running.

"Great! I'm starving," Dahlia said, sitting down at the table.

"Me, too," Rose added.

"I could definitely eat," Lily said.

Liam and Emma fixed plates for the girls, working side by side in a sort of rhythm. They all dug in, eating and talking happily together.

The group was so engrossed in one another that they didn't even notice the man who was observing them through the slats of the fence. He watched for a few more minutes, snapped some pictures, and then dropped his cell phone into his pocket and walked away.

FIFTEEN

After dinner, Sadie and Emma cleaned the kitchen while Liam took the girls into the living room to read them a book.

"They sure seem comfortable together, don't they?" Sadie observed.

"Yeah, it's kind of amazing. Lily was skeptical at first, but Liam won her over pretty quickly. It scares me a little bit, knowing how much we'll all get hurt if this doesn't work out," Emma said with a shake of her head.

"Always the optimist, aren't you?" Sadie laughed.

"It's hard for me not to expect the worst, you know?"

"I don't think Liam is the kind of guy who is out to hurt you and the girls. His feelings seem pretty sincere. He's not like Jacob."

"I don't think he would purposely hurt us. That's not what I mean at all. It's just that… I don't know… I'm afraid of losing him. Since I've let him in, I keep getting these glimpses of myself without him. I don't like it at all, Sadie. I don't know if I would recover again." Emma had finally hit on the truth of the matter.

"Try and have a little faith. I really think things are going to turn out okay for you guys." Sadie hugged Emma tightly. When Emma heard Sadie say it, somehow she believed it might be true.

"You have always known exactly what I need to hear," Emma said.

"Well, I'm beat, and I have to get up early for work tomorrow. I'm going to head home." Sadie kissed her friend on the cheek and they walked to the front door. After another quick hug, Sadie headed upstairs to her apartment.

Emma went back toward the living room and saw Liam lounging on the couch while the girls played happily on the floor next to him. It was such a sweet, contented picture. It looked like a happy family, and she prayed it was there to stay.

SIXTEEN

LATER THE NEXT WEEK, EMMA HURRIED AROUND TRYING TO
ready the girls for spending the night with Sadie, who had
graciously agreed to watch them so she and Liam could have
a quiet evening at his place. He'd moved his belongings into
his new house two days earlier. He'd done everything
himself, and he hadn't taken her up on her offer to help. She
was sure he was just being considerate and didn't want to put
anything more on her already-full plate.

Life with Liam was amazing. He was everything she'd
ever wanted in a man, and things were going splendidly. The
girls were happy, and she was ecstatic. She had never felt so
completely cared for. Liam was truly the "knight in shining
armor" type. He was thoughtful and considerate; his
romantic tendencies took her breath away.

The only problem was the fact that she felt an uneasiness
that couldn't be explained; it was a nervousness that made no
sense. She was in a nearly perfect relationship with a man
who seemed to have walked right out of every woman's
dreams, but despite the perfection, she couldn't shake the
feeling that something was about to go wrong.

"Hurry up, girls! We need to get to Sadie's. Bring your stuff downstairs, please," she called upstairs.

Lily, Dahlia, and Rose ran down the stairs with overnight bags in hand. They were excited to stay at Sadie's, and they didn't need to be told twice.

They walked up the outside stairs to Sadie's apartment, and she opened the front door before they even knocked.

"Be good for Sadie," Emma instructed as she kissed each of them. "I'll see you all tomorrow morning before school."

She thanked her friend, gave everyone a quick hug, and then headed back downstairs to finish dressing before Liam arrived. As she selected her clothing, she thought about Liam's house. She could picture him living in a very masculine home. He hadn't really spoken about it, and he'd been vague when she'd asked him questions. Actually, Liam was vague when it came to most questions that centered on him. Emma didn't think he was being secretive, but she'd learned quickly that he didn't enjoy talking about himself.

She did know he was close to his family, who all lived in Chicago. He had one sister and two nieces, whom he absolutely adored. He couldn't wait to introduce her to them, and they'd already made plans for a trip with the girls over the summer. He hadn't had any serious relationships, and she also knew he didn't open up with most people.

Other than that, Emma decided she didn't know a lot about Liam, though he'd told her that nothing in his past mattered before they met. Under any other circumstances, a statement like that would have made her nervous and uncomfortable, but she trusted him completely. She was certain he wasn't hiding anything.

Emma had just finished dressing when she heard the front door open and shut. Liam didn't knock anymore, and she was happy that he felt comfortable at her home.

"I'm upstairs! I'll be right down," she called loudly.

She walked into the kitchen just as Liam was placing the milk back into the refrigerator, and since she saw no glass, she assumed he'd taken a drink straight from the carton. Smiling to herself, she walked up behind him and wrapped her arms around him. His muscles rippled beneath her fingertips, causing her pulse to quicken.

Turning around, Liam encircled her in his arms as he bent down and hungrily claimed her mouth. She responded eagerly, as she always did. There was so much passion that she often had a hard time containing it all. She'd never experienced a relationship where there was so much give and take in equal measure.

"At this rate, we aren't going to make it to your house for dinner." She giggled between kisses.

"That's fine with me. The house isn't going anywhere," Liam said, gently biting her earlobe.

"I know, but I want to see it, and the girls are at Sadie's for the night. Maybe we can continue this conversation there," she suggested.

"If that's what you want." Liam smiled, but it didn't go all the way to his eyes.

Emma sensed a bit of anxiety in him, but she wasn't sure what it was about. She'd assumed Liam would be excited to show her his new home. She decided she was just imagining something that wasn't there.

"I'm ready if you are." Liam took her hand and led her outside to his car.

Backing out of the driveway, Liam headed down Main Street. He drove a couple of blocks, then made a left onto Russell Street. It was a beautiful night, and Emma was enjoying the drive through town. They drove past Vinnie's and she smiled, thinking of their first date. They'd come a long way since then.

Liam continued on Russell Street and took a right onto

Briar Avenue. It was about that time that Emma began to feel the first prickles of uneasiness. They were headed toward the area of town where she once lived with Jacob, and it was a place Emma avoided. There were too many bad memories.

When Liam turned off Briar Avenue and maneuvered the car onto Rosemary Lane, her palms began to sweat. Her mind was racing, and she was trying to understand why they were driving down her old street. It seemed too coincidental that Liam's new house was there.

Liam glanced at Emma, noticing how tense she had become. Her hands were clenched into fists, and she was staring blankly out the passenger side window. Lost in her own tumultuous thoughts, she said nothing.

Emma was so anxious about being in her old neighborhood that she couldn't even look at Liam. She was closed off inside herself, dealing with things she didn't want to feel, things she hadn't felt in a very long time. The proximity to her old life made her feel as if she'd been locked in a dark room with no way out. Her tension rose and her stomach clenched tightly as the blackness closed in around her.

"Sweetie, you're quiet. Are you okay?" Liam asked.

"Yes," she lied, barely able to form the word.

Liam drove to the end of Rosemary Lane and turned into a driveway. Emma gasped, thinking there must be a mistake.

"What are we doing here?" Her voice registered the panic she felt inside.

"This is my house, Emma," Liam answered evenly.

"This can't be your house. It doesn't make any sense." She wrung her hands in desperation.

"Emma, talk to me," Liam murmured. "Tell me what's wrong."

"This house…." she began, but couldn't go on.

She was suffocating. She had to get out of the car. She needed air.

Fumbling for the door handle, she practically leaped out of the passenger seat of Liam's car. She couldn't bear to be there, but she didn't know what to do. She wanted to run from emotions that she didn't want to feel. She paced back and forth in the driveway beside the car.

Slowly she looked at the house in front of her, and then she glanced to the left. That was where she had lived during her marriage to Jacob. It was just a house, nothing more, but the structure was so completely tied up in memories of hurt and betrayal that even looking at it put her right back there. She'd fought so hard to outrun the pain, but the memories came flooding back—memories she'd buried years before. In that instant, they bobbed to the surface and caused an open wound as if it had only just happened.

She remembered how she'd felt when she discovered Jacob and Veronica's affair, that gut-wrenching pain of betrayal. She and Jacob had shared a family and a life, and it was all a lie. Veronica had lived next door, pretending to be her friend while she was sleeping with Emma's husband. Wave after wave of emotion overtook her, and she collapsed on the driveway and began to sob.

Liam didn't know what to do. He'd known seeing the house wouldn't be easy for Emma, but he'd underestimated what it would do to her. He couldn't bear to see her in pain. He waited for a couple of minutes and gave her space to break down. Then he approached her, knelt on the driveway, and cradled her body in his arms.

Emma continued to weep. She'd never broken down so completely before. She had cried when she'd found out about Jacob and Veronica, and she'd cried when she buried him, realizing her daughters no longer had a father. She had cried even more when her parents died, leaving her alone yet again. But through all of those things, she'd maintained a certain degree of self-control. She'd never fully allowed herself to let go.

In that moment, she wept for all of the times she hadn't. She wept for the times she'd been stronger than she'd wanted to be. She sat in the driveway, engulfed in Liam's strong arms, and cried harder than she'd ever cried in all her life. It was as if someone had opened the floodgates, and she didn't know how to close them. She cried until she couldn't cry anymore.

When the tears finally ran dry, she wiped her eyes and looked at Liam. She was sure he thought she was a complete mental case. She had to say something.

"You're probably wondering why I went into hysterics in your driveway. You must think I'm crazy." She looked up at him.

"I think you're the strongest woman I've ever known, so I know there must be a very good reason that you had that response. I hope you'll tell me," Liam said quietly.

"Liam, this house, your house, was Veronica's house; the same Veronica who was sleeping with my husband right under my nose. And that house right there was where I lived with Jacob." Emma's voice quivered as she pointed toward her old house.

She couldn't believe she'd ever lived that life. She didn't like the woman who had lived in that house. She was weak and too afraid to take control of her own life. Emma never wanted to be that woman again.

And she wouldn't be.

She took a deep breath and pulled herself to a standing position. Now that she was a bit calmer, she felt embarrassed about losing her composure so epically in front of Liam.

"I'm sorry, Liam. I'm sure this wasn't how you envisioned tonight," she apologized.

"Don't ever think you have to apologize for your feelings,"

Liam said as he pulled her close. He felt guilty for her pain. He should never have brought her to his house. He'd witnessed the deep hurt that she so expertly concealed. "Listen, we don't have to stay. I'll take you home and you never have to come back here again."

"No, I think I need to do this. Maybe it'll be good for me to try and get past it." Emma took a deep breath.

"Only if you're sure." Liam's concern was written all over his face.

He knew he should tell her the truth about the connection he had to her past, but he couldn't bring himself to do it. He decided he would tell her later.

"Will you please show me your home?" Emma asked with more determination than she actually felt.

Liam gripped her hand and they walked to the front door. Before opening it, he paused and stared at her. The look on his face was strange, and she wondered what he was about to say.

"Emma, before we go in, I have something I need to tell you," Liam said hesitantly. "It's something I should have said a while ago, but I didn't."

"To be honest, I'm not sure if I can take any more revelations tonight. If it's something bad, maybe you can just keep it to yourself a bit longer," she said nervously.

"It's not bad." Liam began to pace back and forth on his front porch.

"What is it? You're freaking me out," she replied.

"Look, I don't know if this is the right time or not, but I have to say it. Something happened to me the first time I saw you. I'm not someone who rushes into things, but I can't seem to stop myself with you. You've bewitched me or something, and I'm not sure if I like it." Liam ran his hands through his hair in agitation.

Emma's heart was racing. She had no idea where Liam

was headed with his confession, but she automatically assumed the worst. She had the sudden thought that maybe he was trying to tell her that things were moving too quickly between them. She had clearly scared him away with the episode she'd had in his driveway, and he was breaking up with her.

Unaware of her inner thoughts, Liam continued. "I don't know how to say what I want to say. I'm probably not going to make sense, but I'm just going to say it. I love the way you keep me on my toes. I love the way you are with your girls. I love how dedicated you are to your work. I love the way you made me win you over. I love the way you twirl your hair when you're nervous, and I love the way you cry at the end of movies. I love the way you make me feel like I can do anything. Emma, I love you."

Emma thought she might faint. Liam wasn't breaking up with her—he was saying he loved her! She wasn't sure if she was ready for that, but in all honesty, Liam was simply admitting out loud the way she'd secretly felt about him for weeks. She'd known she was headed in that direction, and whether or not she was ready, she felt the same way.

"Emma, I said I love you. Don't leave me hanging here. Say something," Liam pleaded.

Her emotions were on the surface. She'd been sobbing hysterically a few minutes ago, and suddenly all she wanted to do was laugh. The laughter began and it didn't stop. She laughed so hard that she started crying again.

Liam didn't know what to do. He watched as the woman he loved laughed at the declaration of his deepest feelings. That wasn't how it was supposed to go.

Gaining her composure, Emma saw the hurt on Liam's face, and she understood that her reaction hadn't been the best. Liam had said he loved her, and she'd gone off in a fit of laughter. She hadn't properly responded to his words, so she took a breath and tried to think of what she wanted to say. She didn't know exactly where the future might lead, but she knew nothing in the past mattered anymore.

She had let Jacob steal her happiness for far too long; now it was standing right in front of her, and she was ready to reach out and grab it. Jacob and Veronica and all the hurt their deception had caused didn't matter anymore. Nothing mattered except all the emotion that existed between her and Liam. The ghosts who had haunted her for so long couldn't do so anymore. They'd been fully exorcised right there in the driveway. She felt like a thousand pounds had been lifted from her shoulders.

Emma looked at Liam and knew her feelings were real. There was no denying it.

She wrapped her arms around his neck and pulled his face down to hers. Looking into his eyes, she kissed him tenderly before she spoke.

"Liam, I had no intention of falling in love with you. I swore when Jacob died that no one was going to get close enough to hurt me again, but you came along and blew that idea right out of the water. I tried to avoid you. I tried to ignore you, but you wouldn't go away. Little by little, you broke down the walls until I had no choice but to let you in, and I'm glad I did, because I am so in love with you." Her breath shuddered as she finished.

"Well, that's a little more like it." Liam laughed out loud as he grabbed her and crushed her body against his. Their lips met in a heated kiss, and she knew her fate had been sealed.

He picked her up in his arms and carried her across the threshold.

SEVENTEEN

MORNING LIGHT FILTERED THROUGH THE CURTAINS. FEELING A bit disoriented, Emma shifted in the bed beside Liam. Looking around, she tried to place her surroundings, then remembered she had spent the night at Liam's house. The details of the evening before came streaming back. What had begun as the worst night of her life had ended as the best. She and Liam were in love, and nothing was going to get in the way of that.

Quietly, she disentangled her body from Liam's and headed downstairs to his kitchen. She was starving, and Liam would be too. It was only six o'clock in the morning, but Emma's internal clock was set, making her a habitual early riser. She had to be home within an hour to get the girls ready for school, so as much as she would have loved to lie there next to Liam, she had to get moving.

Looking in his refrigerator, she realized there wasn't much to work with. The only things she saw were two eggs, three pieces of lunchmeat, and two slices of provolone. At least there was cheese for the omelet she decided to make. She cracked the eggs into a bowl, found a whisk, and began mixing. She added some salt and pepper, chopped the lunch-meat, gave it a final mix, and then poured it slowly into the sizzling pan.

Omelets were not Emma's favorite things to make, as they required patience, something she was sorely lacking. She tended to flip the omelet too soon, making a mess of it in the process. With a smile, she found herself comparing her own love life to the omelet in front of her. Emma hoped she wasn't "flipping things" too soon with Liam, because she didn't want to make a mess of that.

Taking a breath, she turned the omelet in the pan, relieved that it was sheer perfection. About that time, Liam wandered into the kitchen and wrapped his arms around her. She never got tired of that.

Liam said sleepily, "When I woke up, you were gone. I didn't like it. Then I smelled something wonderful down here and I decided you were forgiven."

"Well that's nice of you," she laughed. "There wasn't much in your refrigerator to work with, so we get to split an omelet."

"Yeah, I haven't been here often enough to stock up on groceries. I'm usually eating at your house these days—not that I'm complaining."

"I noticed that, too. Not that I'm complaining either." She gave him a quick kiss, then handed him a plate of food, and they both sat at the kitchen table.

"No regrets about last night?" Liam asked quietly. "I hope I didn't scare you. I love you, but I don't want you to feel rushed."

"Last night after I told you how I felt, I thought about it for hours. It was a huge step for me. But after revisiting the idea this morning while cooking your omelet, I realized I wouldn't change a thing. I *do* love you, Liam, and I'm not sorry I told you." Emma hoped he understood how serious she was. Their relationship was the best thing that had happened to her in a long time.

Relief flooded Liam's face. He had been convinced that she'd be spooked after she thought about their conversation, and he was happy to hear that wasn't the case.

"So, I have some not-so-great news. I need to go out of town for a few days," he began.

"Out of town? Why?"

"Well, I have some work back in Chicago I have to attend to. I've been using my vacation time while I got situated, but it's time to pull a face-to-face session with the office. My boss called yesterday, and he needs me there to go over a case. You know, a second pair of eyes to be sure he's not missing important details. I wish I didn't have to go." Liam looked at Emma uncertainly.

"I wish you didn't have to go either. I've gotten used to seeing you every day, so I don't think I'm going to like it at all. When do you leave?" She was unable to conceal her disappointment.

"Later this morning. It's short notice, but that's the job. I'll be gone for four days, but I'll call you pretty much a hundred times a day," he said with a laugh.

"You'd better. I'm going to miss the sound of your voice." She leaned in closely to kiss him.

"I'm going to miss a few other things, too," he teased.

She felt a little wave of sadness inside. She hadn't realized just how inseparable they had become. "Hurry back." She held him tightly for a moment.

"As fast as I can," he assured her.

"I love you, Liam."

Smiling, Liam replied, "I love you, too, Emma."

EIGHTEEN

Emma arrived home and determined that she had just enough time for a quick shower and change of clothes before heading upstairs to get the girls. She jumped in and let the steaming water wash over her. There was nothing like a hot shower to get life started in the mornings. Finishing, she hopped out, dried off, and wrapped her hair in a towel. There wouldn't be time for fussing over appearances.

Grabbing a pair of jeans and a purple blouse from the closet, she dressed quickly. She was just about to run out the door to retrieve her daughters when the house phone rang. She picked up on the third ring.

"Hello," she said.

There was no answer. It was exactly the way it had happened the day of the backyard barbeque, and she had no time for games. She was beginning to get irritated.

"Hello," she repeated as her frustration grew. "Is someone there?"

"Tell me where they are," a deep, menacing male voice demanded.

"I'm sorry. I think you must have the wrong number." Emma's frustration gave way to confusion.

"You know where they are, and you'd better tell me. If you don't, you'll be sorry," the man repeated.

Before Emma could respond, the line went dead. It was all very strange and unsettling. She felt certain that it must have been a wrong number, because she didn't recognize the man's voice. It was intimidating, though, and she was a bit shaken.

"You know where they are," he had said. She racked her brain to think of what he might have been talking about. Arriving at no good answer, she concluded that it was indeed a wrong number. There was no other explanation. Grabbing her purse, she headed out the front door, escorted the girls to the school bus, and pushed all thoughts of the random phone call out of her mind.

After that, she headed to Morning Glory. The place was already busy, and there wasn't an open table. Jane had things running smoothly, as usual, but Emma jumped right in to help. The women worked systematically through the morning rush; they were such a great team that they didn't even require words. Once things slowed down, they took a much-needed break before the lunch rush began.

"So, how are things with you and Liam?" Jane asked as she wiped down tables.

"They're great. He's amazing. The girls love him. I love him. Jane, I literally told him I love him. Can you believe that?" Emma beamed.

"You deserve all the happiness in the world, girl."

"But I also keep waiting for the other shoe to drop. I don't know why I can't just relax."

"Because of Jacob," Jane replied in her no-nonsense way. "That jerk never deserved you, and when he betrayed you, I watched you go inside of yourself. You've stayed there all these years. I'm glad Liam has drawn you out. Don't fight that. He's a good man."

"Yes, he is a wonderful man. I guess I'm just having a hard time accepting that good things can happen to me," she answered.

In spite of the fact that everything was going better than she could have imagined, Emma couldn't shake the feeling of doom. She reminded herself of the look on Liam's face as he'd kissed her goodbye that morning. She believed he loved her. She just needed to remember that, and push all the negative thoughts aside.

At the end of the day, Emma headed home to start a load of laundry before the girls arrived. She carried a hamper filled with clothes into the laundry room. Laundry started, she went outside to meet the bus. Her daughters piled off the vehicle and ran to the porch to greet their mother. Everyone began talking at once, and they went inside to begin the afternoon ritual of dinner and homework. Sometimes Emma's afternoons felt a bit like the movie *Groundhog Day*, where she kept doing the same thing over and over again. But that was part of motherhood. It couldn't be helped.

"Mama, I have a reading contest at school this month. Mrs. Vickers said whoever reads the most books can win a prize. I'm going to win," Dahlia said excitedly.

"I'm sure you will." She kissed her daughter on the top of the head. "Why don't you get out the new book I bought for you and get started?"

"Okay, Mama," Dahlia replied as she ran upstairs.

Emma grabbed fresh vegetables from the refrigerator and began chopping. Lily and Rose were busy doing homework, and Dahlia was working on her reading project. The house was strangely quiet for the middle of the afternoon, and she realized that she missed Liam. She jumped as her cell phone rang, and smiled when she saw it was him.

"Hey," she said with a smile. "I was just thinking about you."

"How are you doing? What are you making for dinner? Did the girls get home from school okay?"

She realized he knew their afternoon routine as well as she did. He knew exactly what they would be doing at that very minute. She'd become so used to his presence that his absence left a huge hole in the house.

"Yes, the girls are working on homework. Dahlia is busy reading so she can win the class reading prize. I'm making tacos for dinner." She filled Liam in on the details as she continued to prepare dinner. "You made it to Chicago in one piece?"

"Yep, I landed a few hours ago. I've already been to the office. My boss updated me on the case, and I don't think it'll take that long. I may be home sooner than I thought." Emma could almost hear the smile in his voice. "But I can't believe how much I miss you already."

"Me too. It's quiet here without you. I don't like it one bit," she divulged.

They talked for several more minutes, and Emma didn't want to hang up. She wanted to be connected to him, even if it was only by phone. He hadn't even been gone a full day and she was already having withdrawals. Being around Liam was like a drug, and she was happy to know he felt the same way about her.

Reluctantly they said goodbye to one another, with Liam promising he would call the next morning.

Later that evening, after the girls were tucked into bed and the last load of laundry was in the dryer for the night, she headed to her room to unwind. She watched some mindless reality television for a bit and her eyelids grew heavy. She was about to turn off the TV and go to sleep when the phone rang. The number read "Unavailable." Normally she wouldn't answer it, but she thought it might be Liam calling from a different number.

"Hello," she said.

There was no answer, but she heard the distinct sound of someone breathing on the other end. It was exactly what had happened twice before on her house phone. This time, though, it was her cell phone. She didn't give her number out to many people. Goose bumps began to prickle her skin.

"Hello." Emma felt uneasy as the realization dawned that a random person had gotten her cell phone number.

"Hello, Emma." The strange male voice disturbed her.

She had a sense of recognition. She had heard the voice before. It was the man who had called her house phone earlier that morning. It was the voice that had said, "You know where they are." She had been so sure it was a wrong number, but now he was calling her cell phone.

"Who is this?" she demanded.

"You don't recognize me, Emma? We spoke this morning. You need to tell me what you know. Do you believe I'm serious now?" the menacing man continued.

"I don't know what you're talking about. What am I supposed to tell you?" She worked hard to control the fear in her voice.

She had no idea who the man was or why he was calling her. She didn't know what he wanted. He seemed to know her name, though, and that was enough to scare her.

"You're going to tell me where they are, Emma, or you will not enjoy the consequences."

"I don't know what you're talking about," she insisted.

"You should ask Liam O'Reilly. I'll be in touch."

The phone clicked as the man hung up. Emma had no idea what to do. It clearly wasn't a wrong number. The stranger had said her name, and he brought up Liam. He knew who she was. He knew about Liam. Suddenly, she was terrified. If he had her number, he probably knew where she lived. She was in some kind of danger, although she had no idea why.

She looked out her bedroom window at the dark street below. She didn't see anyone, but she had the feeling of being watched. Maybe he was out there, sitting in the dark. For the first time in years, she was afraid inside of her own house.

She paced the floor of her bedroom, unsure what to do next. She thought maybe she should call the police, but she didn't know what she would tell them. The man hadn't done anything except make a call to her phone. It wasn't exactly a police matter. Normally she would just call Sadie, but she was out of town visiting her mom. She considered calling Liam, but he was all the way in Chicago, and she didn't want him to worry. Knowing him, he would race back immediately if he even suspected that she might be in danger.

Emma refused to place his job in jeopardy because she was afraid. She wouldn't interfere in his life just because she'd been spooked by a phone call. She was going to handle it on her own. She was a competent adult, and she could take care of herself.

She crept downstairs to check the doors and windows. Everything was locked up tight, but she was still afraid. Emma returned to her room and crawled into bed. For the first time since she was a young girl, she decided to leave the light on, but sleep didn't come for a very long time. When it finally did, it was a fitful, restless sleep.

She dreamed she was alone in the forest. It was dark and cold, and she was being pursued by a stranger. She couldn't see his face, but she heard his voice. He called her name as he chased her, his footsteps growing closer and closer. He tracked her through the trees. She ran as fast as she could, dressed only in her nightgown, her bare feet cut and bleeding from the forest debris below.

She couldn't outrun him. Her lungs were on fire, and he was gaining on her. Her nightgown caught on a tree branch and ripped in half. She tried to grab the thin fabric to cover herself, but she lost her footing. Stumbling, she fell to the forest floor. Closing in, the man reached down and grabbed her wrist. Panic seized her as she let out a scream, but it was too late.

Emma bolted upright in bed as the dream let her go. Sunlight filtered in through the windows, and she realized it was morning.

NINETEEN

Emma rolled out of bed exhausted. The previous night had been terrible, and she didn't hold out much hope for the day ahead. She had barely slept, and the little slumber she'd managed was restless. She was spooked by the stranger's phone call, and she was trying to come to grips with the fact that someone was stalking her. Things like that just didn't happen to ordinary people like her.

The most worrisome thought was that the stranger had her personal phone number, and he knew her name. It made her wonder what else he knew. Perhaps he had been following her and therefore knew where she lived. Maybe he knew where her daughters went to school. He knew Liam's name, and that he spent a lot of time there. A million questions ran through her head, and the uneasy feeling took up residence. She'd been violated and made to feel unsafe in her own home, and it angered her.

She debated on telling Liam about the phone calls. Part of her wanted to tell him, knowing he would race home to protect her. Another part, the one she'd relied on for years, told her she was completely capable of taking care of herself.

Old habits die hard, and the independent side won out in the end.

She rationalized that the stalker probably wouldn't call again; therefore, there was no need to make an issue of it. Convinced that was true, she readied herself for the day. She tried her best to believe that things were not as bad as they had seemed the night before.

Later that morning, she was at work brewing a fresh cup of coffee for a customer when she had the distinct feeling that she was being watched. Her instincts were on high alert, so she peered out the large windows in the front of the shop. To her surprise, no one was there. She scolded herself for losing her composure, and knowing she needed to get a firm grasp on her nerves before she completely lost touch with reality.

Just as she was about to go back to work, she spotted the same car she'd believed was following her a few weeks ago. Standing beside the car was the same man. He was again dressed completely in black, wearing black sunglasses and a black ball cap, leaning on his car casually.

Beckland was a small town, and Emma recognized most of the people in it. She couldn't say that about the stranger, and the fact that he'd been in close proximity to her twice made her uneasy. She'd learned a long time ago to trust her gut, and that's what she had to do.

Deciding she was going to find out who he was and what he wanted, Emma stalked out the front door of the coffee shop and headed in his direction. When he saw her coming, he adjusted his ball cap, jumped into his car, and quickly started the ignition. Before she reached him, he pulled out of the parking space and sped away with screeching tires.

If she had been unsure before, there was no question that the man was up to no good, and he was definitely targeting her. Something told her he was the man who had made the phone calls as well. In spite of the revelation, she had no idea what to do with the information. She had no idea who he was, and she hadn't reacted quickly enough to get his license plate number.

Frustrated, Emma trudged back inside of the shop. Jane looked at her questioningly, but she wasn't in the mood to answer questions. Without a word, she headed to the back room to work in her office. As she flopped into the chair behind her desk, she wondered if it was time to tell Liam about the phone calls and the suspicious man. As much as she wanted to unburden herself, something held her back. She didn't care for the idea of being viewed as a helpless woman. She'd been in charge of her own life before he came along, and she wanted to remain self-sufficient. If matters got worse, she would tell him then. She'd just be extra cautious for the next few days.

Emma's traumatic night was catching up with her, and she felt a headache coming on. She needed to go home and lie down for a bit before the girls arrived. Jane agreed to handle things at the shop, but Emma knew from the look on her friend's face that she was concerned.

Unlocking the front door of her house, Emma was greeted by quietness. Her head felt like it was going to explode, and all she could think about was sleeping. The girls wouldn't be home for two hours, so she locked the door behind her and went upstairs to her room. Opening the medicine cabinet, she popped ibuprofen into her mouth, washed the capsules down with water, and crawled into bed. She closed her eyes and willed the medicine to do the trick. She quickly drifted off to sleep, but dreams overtook her mind once again.

She ran as she was pursued by an unknown man. She couldn't see his face, but his breath came fast and hard behind her as he chased her down a darkened alley. She ran as fast as her legs would carry her, but she felt him gaining on her. She gasped, breathing hard as he ruthlessly pursued her. He was close behind. Suddenly he reached out and grabbed her hair, causing her to tumble onto the pavement below. She opened her mouth to scream, but no sound came out. There was no escape. His face was shadowed by the night.

She had no idea who he was, but he knew her. "Hello, Emma. We finally meet." His voice made her blood run cold.

The alarm on her phone beeped and tore her from the frightening dream. She fumbled to turn it off, grateful for the interruption of the terror in her mind. Thankfully, her headache was gone, although she didn't feel rested. She trudged downstairs and walked outside just as the bus rounded the corner.

Lying on her front porch was a bouquet of dead roses.

TWENTY

With a racing heart, Emma bent down and grabbed the dead flowers. There was no getting around the fact that the latest scare was not a coincidence. Whoever the man was, he was trying to frighten her, and he was doing a spectacular job. She tossed the dead flowers into the trash can at the end of the driveway, plastered a fake smile on her face, and went to the curb to retrieve her children from the bus.

Her daughters' lighthearted moods were exactly what she needed to get her mind off what was going on. She didn't want them to know anything was wrong, and the last thing she wanted was for them to feel unsafe. Their well-being was her only concern, and she would not have that taken away by a stalker with a misplaced vendetta.

As they began their afternoon ritual of homework, Emma decided she just wasn't up for the drudgery of cooking. The girls let out a cheer when she told them she was ordering pizza. She called in the order and headed to the laundry room to start a load. Sometimes it felt like her entire life was made up of food preparation and dirty clothes.

When her cell phone rang, she cringed at the sound. If it was the stalker again, she didn't know what she was going to do. Looking at the display, she sighed with relief when she saw it was Liam.

She tried her best to sound cheerful. "Hey, how are you doing?"

"Great. Things are going well. I have some good news for you." Liam's voice was a balm for her frazzled nerves.

"What's the news?" She was grateful for anything that would distract her from the current situation.

"The news is that I'll be home tomorrow, earlier than planned, and I can't wait to see you."

"Oh, I'm so glad to hear that." She couldn't hide the relief in her voice, and she nearly burst into tears. She was having a hard time keeping it together.

"Honey, is everything okay? You don't sound like yourself," Liam inquired.

"I'm fine," she lied. "I just miss you."

"Me too. I had no idea how hard it would be to leave you and the girls. Apparently I can't even take being away from you for two days without turning into a pile of mush." Liam chuckled on the other end of the phone.

"Well, I don't mind. I'll be really happy to see you." She meant the words with everything in her.

They talked a little more, and then the girls asked to speak with him. It was cute to hear them on the phone, knowing they missed him as well. They said their goodbyes, and as they hung up, she was grateful that he would be back in Beckland soon.

Later that night, the girls were tucked into bed and the last load of laundry was nearly completed. She was cleaning up the kitchen when her phone chimed, informing her that she had a text message. She smiled to herself, certain Liam was texting her to say good night. She grabbed the phone and clicked the message icon.

Her heart pounded when she saw it wasn't from Liam but an unavailable number. With trepidation, she opened the message. It was a photo of Emma and her children in the backyard. Beneath the picture were the words *"I see you."*

She swallowed hard and forced herself to study the picture more closely. It was taken through the slats of her fence. Someone had taken a picture of them when they were totally unaware. The feeling of complete violation ran deep. The stalker had been in close proximity to her family, and she'd been totally oblivious.

In a moment of anger, she contemplated deleting the message. She just wanted it to be gone. The stranger had tainted her memory of a special day with her family.

After catching her breath, she realized she might need it as evidence, so she saved the text instead. She knew she had to tell Liam everything. She would be stupid to keep denying it and pretending she could handle it on her own. The situation was far bigger than she'd believed it to be. That picture was proof that she needed help. The man had been far too close to her family, and they were in very real danger.

She checked the doors and windows throughout the large house. Once she was satisfied that they were securely locked, she went upstairs to her room. She hated feeling so unsafe, and she was angry and frustrated that a complete stranger had managed to rob her of her security.

She was too worked up to sleep, and she was unable to stop her mind from racing. She was going to tell Liam everything, but she wanted to do it without sounding needy. Then again, perhaps her pride didn't even matter anymore. She did need his help. She hoped he wouldn't view it as a sign of weakness.

Seeing that picture had been enough to convince Emma

that her family was in danger. She would be a negligent fool to stick her head in the sand and pretend everything was fine. She would tell Liam the very next day, just as soon as he was home.

With that knowledge in her mind, she turned off the lights and tried her best to get some sleep.

TWENTY-ONE

ONCE AGAIN, EMMA'S NIGHT WAS PLAGUED BY HORRIBLE, terrifying dreams. She hadn't slept well in days, and it was catching up with her. She was exhausted and especially grumpy as she woke the girls for school. She did her best not to lose her temper with them, and to their credit, they made things easy. Perhaps they gauged her mood and came to the conclusion that it wasn't the best day to test their mother.

They obediently got out of bed, dressed quickly, and seated themselves at the kitchen table by the time Emma finished her shower.

"Mama, are you okay?" Rose inquired as Emma scraped scrambled eggs onto her plate.

"Yeah, baby, I'm fine." Emma tried to sound lighthearted. "I just didn't sleep very well, and I'm kind of tired today."

"You should take a nap, Mommy." Dahlia sounded concerned.

"Yeah, Mom, you look tired. Why don't you stay home from work and get some rest?" Lily added. "Jane won't mind."

"You girls are sweet to be concerned for me, but don't

worry. I'm fine." Emma plastered a smile on her face in order to be convincing.

She needed to pull herself together. She was the adult. It wasn't her daughters' job to be worried about her. She didn't want them to know that being home alone was the last thing she wanted to do under the current circumstances.

Emma deserved an Academy Award for her performance during the remainder of breakfast. She convinced the girls that Mom was perfectly fine, and they kissed her goodbye and headed to the bus. She grabbed her purse and headed next door to work, locking the front door securely behind her.

She settled into her office at Morning Glory, sorting through invoices when a familiar presence filled the room. She didn't even need to look up to know it was Liam standing in the doorway. Emma had never been so glad to see someone in her life. Just knowing he was there made her feel safe, and she was so thankful that he was home. She sprang from her desk and ran across the room toward him, flinging her body into his arms. She never wanted to be away from him again.

"Well that's quite the welcome home." He laughed as he ran his fingers through Emma's hair.

"I missed you so much. Please tell me you don't have to go again anytime soon." She heard the desperation in her voice, but she didn't even care.

"Hey, wait a minute. What's wrong, Emma?" Liam pulled away and forced her to look at him. "This is more than just missing me. Sit down and tell me what's going on."

There was no hiding from Liam. He could see right through her. The time for stalling was over. She had to come clean.

"Well, there is something I haven't told you. But you have to promise you won't be mad at me for not telling you sooner. It's just that counting on someone to help me doesn't come naturally. My first instinct is to help myself, so that's what I did." Emma wanted to lay the groundwork for what she was about to reveal.

"Emma, I'm not going to be mad. Just tell me what's going on, please." Liam's face was filled with concern.

"Do you remember when we had the barbecue in the backyard with Sadie? Remember that weird phone call I got? The one where I heard the person breathing?"

"Yeah, I remember. What about it?"

"Well, over the next few weeks, I got more of them. I knew there was someone on the line because I could hear breathing, but no one ever answered. I just ignored them, thinking it was a wrong number." Emma felt nervous even recounting the story.

"Go on," Liam encouraged.

"The first night you were in Chicago, I got another phone call. By then I was irritated, but that time was different. The person on the phone said my name. He asked where 'they' are, and I have no idea what that means. He said there was something I wasn't telling him. He also said you knew something about it." Emma swallowed hard and paced the floor of her office as she relived the story.

"The next day at work, I saw a man watching me through the windows. I had seen him before when I was walking. I thought he was following me, but I ignored it. The same guy was watching me again. So I went outside to confront him—"

"Confront him?"

"Well, yeah."

"Are you out of your mind? What were you thinking?" Liam ran his hands through his hair in obvious frustration.

"You promised not to get mad, Liam. Just please let me finish telling this without interrupting."

"Sorry. Go on." Liam looked more than a little impatient.

"Anyway, when he saw me coming, he jumped in his car and took off. I didn't get his license plate number. I also found dead roses on my front porch. Later that night, I got a text message. It was a picture taken through my backyard fence. It said 'I see you.'"

"What?" he fumed.

"Liam, I don't know what this is about, but I'm afraid. I've been having nightmares, and I haven't slept well in days. I'm afraid to be home alone. When I'm there, I'm constantly checking the doors and windows to be sure they're locked. I'm going a little crazy, and I don't know what to do. Do you know something about this?" Emma felt the tears brimming in her eyes, and she tried hard to hold them in.

Liam sat there for a few minutes in silence. His jaw was clenched, and she could tell he was trying to process her words. He didn't look at her, and she thought he must be angry because he wouldn't speak.

"Are you mad at me? Would you please say something? You're making me nervous," Emma said quietly.

"First of all, I am not mad at you. I'm frustrated with you for keeping secrets from me, but I understand. You're not used to someone being there to help you. I'm trying to keep that in mind as I continue to be frustrated."

"Look, I'm sorry. If I could go back, I would have told you the first time I started to get nervous. But I'm telling you now. I don't know what to do about this, and I need your help."

"Well, you have my help, whether you want it or not. I am definitely taking this seriously, and I will protect you and the girls with my life. Until we know what's going on, I don't want you to be alone. I'm moving some of my things into your house today, and I'm staying there until we figure out who this creep is and what he wants," Liam said with authority.

Whatever Emma's misgivings might have been about him staying at her house, she pushed them aside when she saw his jaw set with determination. The only thing that mattered was her daughters' safety, and she would do whatever was needed to ensure it. If that meant Liam stayed in their home, then so be it.

"You can stay at the house. I'm not going to argue with you, but I don't want the girls to be afraid. We need to come up with a reason why you're there." As she spoke, she formulated the plan in her head. "We'll tell them your house is being painted and you need a place to stay."

"Tell them whatever you need to, but I'm staying there. I will not let anything happen to you or to them. I promise you that." Liam reached across the desk to grab her hands. "I will find out who this guy is."

Emma's heart practically leaped out of her chest with relief and love for Liam. His fiercely protective nature was one of the things she loved most about him. The knots that had been in her stomach for the past several days slowly began untwisting. The tension went out of her shoulders.

"You finish up your day here at work. I'm going over to my place to grab the things I'll need. Are you leaving early or staying until the girls get home? I'm going to walk with you," Liam said.

"Walk with me? Liam, it's like ten steps from here to the house. I'm pretty sure I can manage," Emma laughed.

"When I say I don't want you alone, I mean I don't want you alone at all. Not even for a second. Someone has threatened you. You have to take this seriously. We're not arguing over this."

"All right. I'll be finished here at three thirty. That's when the girls get home from school."

"Then I'll be back before three thirty. Do not leave until I get here," Liam declared.

He leaned down to kiss her goodbye before heading out the door. If she weren't so afraid of the stranger and his threats, she might have been irritated at Liam's overprotectiveness. As it was, she was so spooked by the situation that she was looking forward to being able to relax with Liam on the case.

TWENTY-TWO

TRUE TO HIS WORD, LIAM RETURNED TO MORNING GLORY AT three o'clock. He asked Emma for the house key and unloaded his belongings from the car. She had the fleeting thought that she should make a copy of the key since he would be there for the unforeseeable future.

A few weeks before, the idea of Liam moving into her house would have sent her into a full-blown panic attack, but now she was actually surprised at how calm she felt about the whole thing. Living under the same roof would seriously change their relationship, but she hoped it would change in a good way. With all that had happened, she was just grateful he was there.

"Liam is acting a little possessive, isn't he, Em?" Jane asked with a concerned look on her face. She obviously had no idea about the reason for Liam's protectiveness.

"There are some things going on that I haven't told you about, Jane. I don't have the mental energy to talk about it right now, but trust me when I say Liam is only doing what is necessary." She'd always been able to share her problems with Jane, but she just didn't have it in her at that moment.

"Well, I won't pry into your business, but I hope you know you can tell me anything," Jane replied kindly.

"I promise I'll tell you. I just can't go into it again right now. It's too hard to talk about," Emma said as her anxiety warred inside of her.

"No rush, Em. I'm here whenever you're ready."

Thirty minutes later, Liam arrived to escort her home from Morning Glory. For about the millionth time in the last couple of days, Emma wished Sadie was there. She was visiting her parents in New York, and she would be gone for two more weeks. Emma missed her dreadfully. She hadn't called to tell her what was going on because she didn't want to mess up her visit. Knowing Sadie, she would have cut her vacation short to come home and help solve the problem.

Liam and Emma waited on the porch for the school bus to arrive. The girls ran toward them and squealed when they saw Liam was back. They had missed him, and it was obvious from the smile on his face that the feeling was mutual. Emma hoped their temporary living situation wouldn't turn into an issue. It would definitely test their relationship.

"It's so good to see you, girls." Liam pulled them close in a big hug. "I sure did miss you."

"We missed you too." Rose planted a kiss on Liam's cheek.

"Not as much as Mom did. She's been moping around the house for days," Lily said, glancing toward her mother with a worried expression on her face.

"I have not been moping." Emma knew her oldest daughter had seen right through her act. She knew something was wrong.

"Who has homework? I'm here to help." Liam tried to circumvent the issue and change the subject, and Emma loved him for it.

"You can help me," Dahlia replied. "I have a spelling test tomorrow. You ask me the words and I'll spell them for you."

"Perfect. Maybe I'll learn something too."

Liam and Dahlia settled into the living room for a spelling quiz, and Rose and Lily headed to the kitchen for snacks. Emma fumbled through the pantry in an effort to decide what to make for dinner. She was distracted by trying to settle on an explanation for their new living situation, worried the girls would grow used to Liam being there and then it would change again. She also knew they needed his protection, but she didn't want them to know that.

"Is Liam staying for dinner, Mom?" Lily asked, looking up from her social studies homework.

Emma decided that was the lead-in she needed, so she called everyone into the kitchen. Once they were settled, she dove in with the news.

"Lily, you asked if Liam was staying for dinner, and the short answer is yes. The longer answer is that Liam will be staying with us for a while. His new house is being painted, and he needs a place to stay."

Emma found that the words came quite easily. She didn't make a habit of lying to her daughters, but there was an exception to every rule. The almost-truth came from a place of fierce protectiveness for her children, and she would do anything to keep them safe.

"So he's going to stay here?" Dahlia questioned.

"For a while. We don't want him inhaling paint fumes, do we? I didn't think you girls would mind."

"Oh, we don't mind at all, Mommy," Dahlia said excitedly.

"Yeah, that will be kind of cool," Lily agreed.

"Where's Liam going to sleep, Mama?" Rose's innocent question took her mother by surprise.

"Well, Liam is going to sleep in the, uh… maybe in…,"

Emma stammered, unsure of how to answer without inviting an entirely different discussion.

"On the couch," Liam finished for her. "I'm going to sleep on the couch."

Emma was grateful that he'd rescued her. The last thing she wanted to discuss was adult sleeping arrangements. What she really wanted was for the conversation to be over.

"I appreciate you girls letting me hang out here," Liam said. "I think it'll be different, but it might be fun." He had a way with the girls that Emma admired.

"We agree," Dahlia replied with a grin.

"I have an idea, girls. Why don't we fix dinner tonight while Mom goes upstairs to take a nice long hot bath? She looks tired."

"Yeah, Mom, go on," Lily agreed. "We'll fix dinner tonight."

"I guess I could do that. If you're sure…." Emma was taken aback. She wasn't used to having someone else at the helm, and she certainly wasn't accustomed to relaxing in the middle of the afternoon.

"Emma, I'm sure. If I'm staying here, I'm going to help out. Don't worry, I won't burn anything." Liam gave her a teasing smile.

After more reassurance that Liam had everything under control, Emma headed upstairs. She had anticipated the conversation about Liam's new living arrangements being awkward, but it hadn't been that way at all. The girls were on board, and they were all in the process of making dinner while she headed up to luxuriate in a bath. If that was the status quo, she could definitely get used to it.

She went into the bathroom, turned on the hot water, and poured bubble bath into the tub. She let the water fill to capacity and slid inside. It felt wonderful to just be still for a few minutes. With everything going on, she'd been on edge for days. As the hot water worked its magic, the tension left her body. She knew she could de-stress with Liam in charge.

She placed her weary head against the back of the tub and closed her eyes, trying to clear her mind and fully surrender to the relaxation. The sleeplessness of the previous days began to catch up with her, and she slowly drifted off to sleep.

When she woke, she was surprised to find that she was no longer in the bathtub. Instead, she was lying in her bed, wrapped in a large fluffy bath towel and covered by the plush blanket that she usually kept at the bottom of the bed. The clock on the nightstand read 9:00 p.m. It had been four o'clock in the afternoon when she'd gone upstairs for her bath. She vaguely remembered falling asleep, but she didn't remember getting out of the tub and climbing into bed. She must have been sleepwalking, and she'd somehow lost five hours of her life.

Emma grabbed her robe and walked down the hall, anticipating the chaos she was about to encounter as a result of sleeping away the afternoon. She had no doubt that the girls were running around, wild and crazy, not yet ready for bed. She didn't know if they'd eaten dinner, and she hated to think of the mess she was going to find in the rest of the house.

As she walked past the girls' rooms, she stopped dead in her tracks. All three of her daughters were sound asleep. They were each in clean pajamas, and they'd been expertly tucked into bed. She had no idea what was going on.

She walked downstairs into the kitchen and was shocked to find that it had been immaculately cleaned. It was practically sparkling. Dishes were washed, counters were spotless, and coffee was made for the following morning.

Amazed, she wandered into the living room and found

Liam lounging on the couch watching a basketball game. She felt like she'd entered an alternate universe.

"Hey, sleepyhead," Liam said with a grin.

Emma flopped down on the couch next to him. "Maybe you can tell me where the last five hours of my life have gone?"

"You went upstairs to take a bath, and the girls and I fixed some chicken alfredo. They really like to cook, by the way. They seemed a little surprised that I knew what I was doing. After that, we finished homework—they only argued with me a little bit. Then I sent them upstairs to take their baths, I read them all a story, and I tucked them into bed. Once that was finished, I cleaned up the kitchen and decided to watch some basketball," Liam answered matter-of-factly. "Oh yeah, there's a plate of food for you in the oven."

Liam went to the kitchen and returned with a plate of chicken alfredo, warmed to the perfect temperature, along with a fork and napkin on a tray, placing everything in front of Emma. She was still in shock. He really was too good to be true. She took a bite and closed her eyes in appreciation as the delicious food tickled her taste buds. Liam was an amazing cook.

"You did all of this while I was asleep? I must have been completely out of it. I don't even remember getting out of the bathtub." Emma was even more confused than she had been before.

"Technically you didn't get out of the tub. When dinner was ready, I came upstairs to let you know, and I found you sound asleep. Your water was ice cold, and I was worried you were going to drown, so I grabbed a towel, lifted you out of the bath tub, wrapped you up, and carried you to bed. I didn't want to wake you, since you clearly needed sleep. The girls and I ate dinner, finished all of the chores for the night, and then they went to bed."

"Liam—"

"Oh yeah, and I also folded the load of laundry you had in the dryer and started another load," he finished.

Emma couldn't believe what she was hearing. Liam had completed a full day's worth of chores. If she hadn't already been head over heels for him, that would have been her tipping point.

"You're amazing. I don't even have words right now. I'm just so glad you're here." Emma's eyes filled with tears.

"Does that mean I don't have to sleep on the couch tonight?" Liam had a mischievous look in his eyes.

"You most definitely do not have to sleep on the couch tonight." Emma took his hand and led him up the stairs toward the bedroom.

TWENTY-THREE

She slept better than she had in days. She was afraid she would have trouble falling asleep after her five-hour nap, but she was apparently so sleep-deprived that it wasn't a problem.

When she woke the next morning, Liam was gone. She grabbed her robe and padded down the stairs, finding him on the couch, sound asleep. She had no idea how long he'd been there, but she knew he wanted the girls to think he had slept there the entire night.

She poured herself a cup of coffee, grabbed the ingredients for breakfast, and then went upstairs to wake the girls. Unbelievably, they got up with only a minimal amount of grumbling. As they worked on getting dressed for school, she headed back downstairs to finish cooking, seeing Liam folding the blankets on the couch.

"Good morning," he said as he kissed her. "I snuck down here an hour or so ago just in case the girls got up earlier than I did. Your couch is pretty comfortable, and I didn't want them to find me upstairs. It would ruin our good reputation."

"Great idea. We wouldn't want to get a bad reputation," Emma said with a smile.

"What can I help you do in here?" Liam grabbed a coffee mug from the kitchen cupboard and filled it to the top.

"You took care of dinner last night, so breakfast is on me. You can have the morning off." Emma continued cooking the scrambled eggs.

"In that case, I'm going to go shower. I'll be down in a few minutes."

Before long, the girls were seated at the table devouring their breakfast. They ate well, carried their dishes to the sink, grabbed their backpacks, and rushed out just in time to catch the bus.

As Emma was cleaning up the kitchen, Liam came downstairs.

"I have food for you if you're hungry," she said.

"I'm starving, thanks," Liam replied, digging heartily into the plate she placed before him.

"It was nice having you here last night. That's the safest I've felt in a long time, so thank you." She looked Liam in the eyes to be sure he knew how much she meant the words.

"There's no place I'd rather be, Emma. Besides, protecting you gives me a great excuse to shack up with you."

"Oh really? Is that what we're doing? Shacking up?" She feigned irritation.

"Well, it looks that way to me." Liam shrugged.

"Well, if last night is any indication of what 'shacking up' with you is like, then I'm all for it," she said with a giggle.

The carefree moment was interrupted by the ringing of Emma's phone. She grabbed it from the counter and cringed when she saw the display register "Unavailable." She'd been holding out hope that the stalker had grown tired of harassing her. Liam obviously noticed the crestfallen look on her face as she answered the phone, his brow furrowing.

"Hello," she said tentatively.

"Good morning, Emma," the stranger said. "I noticed you had a house guest last night."

"What do you want? Why don't you just leave me alone?" she demanded angrily.

Liam grabbed the phone from her hand. "Who is this?" After a couple of seconds, he irritably hit the End button. "There's no one there. He already hung up." Liam angrily ran his hands through his hair.

"I hate knowing I'm being watched. What does he want from me? I don't know what he's looking for." Emma was on the verge of tears.

Liam wrapped his arms around her and rubbed her back in soothing circular motions. "Baby, I'm going to find out who he is and what he wants. I promise."

"I don't know how much longer I can live like this," Emma said with a shaking voice.

"Listen, why don't you go upstairs and get ready to go? I'm going to work from here today, so I can walk you next door and then come back."

She obediently went upstairs, feeling like a deflated balloon. Going to work was the last thing she wanted to do, but she didn't have a choice. She was expecting a large shipment, and she couldn't leave Jane alone to deal with it. Besides, she hoped working would keep her mind off what was going on.

Once she was ready, Liam escorted her next door. She felt like a child being walked to school by her parent. It seemed ridiculous that she had to be walked ten feet from her house to work, but Liam insisted, and she didn't have the energy for an argument. She was no longer in control of her own life. Liam kissed her goodbye and promised to come get her at the end of the day.

Jane looked at Emma inquisitively as she entered

Morning Glory, but she didn't ask any questions. Emma smiled weakly and headed back to her office. She shut the door, collapsed at her desk, then broke down and cried.

ONCE SHE HAD herself under control, she readied the stock room for the shipment that would arrive any moment. The key was that she had to stay busy. She couldn't dissolve into tears every five minutes, even if she felt like it.

"Emma, the truck is here," Jane said as she poked her head through the door of the stock room.

"Things are ready here. Tell the delivery guy to bring it on back." Emma refused to meet Jane's eyes. If she saw compassion and concern there, she would lose it again.

The rest of the afternoon crawled by at a snail's pace. She kept busy, but the hands on the clock seemed to be at a standstill. Finally three thirty arrived, and Liam was there to walk her home.

They met the bus as they'd done the day before, started the girls on their homework, and began making dinner. Liam was helping Lily with a math problem when his cell phone rang. He glanced at the display, excused himself, and went outside to take the phone call. A few minutes later, he trudged back inside the house looking grim.

"Emma, can I speak with you for a second, please?" Liam headed up the stairs and she followed. She couldn't imagine what was going on.

"What's up?" She shut the bedroom door behind them.

"That was a call from work. I need to send a few files to my boss, and they're on my home computer. He needs them tonight." Liam raked his hands through his hair. She couldn't help but note that he did it when he was nervous and frustrated.

"Okay…." Emma had no idea why that was such a big deal.

"Look, I don't want to leave you alone, and it's going to take me a couple of hours to finish my notes on the files and send them. I think you and the girls should come with me."

"Is that all? I thought it was something serious," she replied with a wave of her hand. "We'll be fine here for a couple of hours. Besides, if the kids don't get to bed on time, they'll be monsters in the morning, and trust me when I say you do not want to see that."

"Emma—"

"I promise the doors will all be locked. Besides, you're only across town if I need you," she insisted.

Liam was unconvinced, but he had little choice in the matter. He had work to do, and he needed to do it. She assured him that they would be perfectly fine inside the securely locked house. He decided he wouldn't leave until after the girls were in bed.

When he left, he doled out strict instructions to keep everything locked and not answer the door. Emma felt like a child, but she tried to be understanding of his stress level. He was nervous about leaving for a couple of hours, and she felt guilty for putting him under so much pressure.

She settled into bed and decided to watch a movie and wait for Liam to return. As she flipped through the channels, she noticed *Casablanca* was just starting. It was one of her favorite old movies, and it would keep her occupied for a while. It was romantic, and it would be the perfect distraction.

She'd made it about halfway through the movie when her phone rang. Assuming it was Liam, she answered on the first ring, quickly realizing her mistake.

"You're home alone, I see," the stranger said.

"What do you want?" She didn't know what else to say to

the man. She wished she knew the magic words that would stop the mess.

"Stop playing dumb with me. You know what I want. You're testing my patience. Just tell me where to find them."

Emma detected a frantic sound in his voice that she hadn't heard before. That was a bad sign. He was obviously desperate for information that he thought she had.

"I told you I don't know what you're talking about," she responded desperately.

"You know more than you're saying. Your boyfriend knows too. Ask him. There are a lot of things you don't know about Liam O'Reilly." The man's voice sent chills down her spine.

"What don't I know about Liam? Why won't you tell me?"

"I'm warning you. Cooperate or you'll be sorry," the stranger said before the line went dead.

Emma thought about the man's words. He said there were things she didn't know about Liam. What things? How were they connected to the phone calls? She had a hard time believing Liam was harboring secrets that would put her life in danger.

A million thoughts were swirling around in her head when her phone rang again. She glanced at the display and breathed a sigh of relief when she saw it was Liam. He said he was on his way home and that he would use his key to come in.

When he returned, he knew something was wrong. "What happened?"

"He called again. He knew you weren't here, which means he's watching me," she replied.

"What did he say this time?" Liam worked to control his anger.

"He said he was running out of patience and that I have what he wants. He also said there are a lot of things I don't know about you." Emma searched Liam's face for reassurance that it wasn't true.

Liam didn't appear shocked that the man had mentioned him, and his lack of surprise seemed strange. She had no idea what was going on, but what if it was somehow tied to Liam? The last thing she wanted was to believe that was true, but she had a bad feeling. She had to find out who the stranger was and why he was targeting her. She also needed to know if Liam was somehow involved.

"Emma, I will take care of you. Please don't worry." He wrapped his arms around her.

She tried to relax into them, but her intuition was screaming that Liam knew something he wasn't telling her. His intentions were good, and she loved him fiercely, but her gut told her something was wrong. As much as she didn't want to invade his privacy, she had to know if it was true. Her life and the lives of her children depended on it.

TWENTY-FOUR

Emma woke with a plan securely formulated. She'd thought about it all night long, and she'd finally figured out how she could get away from Liam long enough to do some digging into his past. She'd planned to take the day off, but going to her office would allow her to surf the internet for information on Liam and his FBI career without him peering over her shoulder. She had no idea what she was looking for, and she wasn't sure what she would find. She prayed Liam wasn't involved in something that had put them in danger, because she didn't know what she would do if he was.

Emma didn't want to snoop into Liam's past, but he hadn't left her much choice. He wasn't exactly forthcoming with personal information, and if a case of his was connected to the man who was harassing her, she deserved to know.

Liam was still sleeping, and that was for the best. The less she had to interact with him, the better. She didn't want him to pick up on her anxiety, which was at an all-time high. Besides, she was a terrible liar, and he would see right through her.

She fixed the girls a quick breakfast, then hurried them

out of the house and onto the bus. Liam was still sound asleep, so she left him a note saying she had some work to do at the coffee shop. He would probably be angry that she didn't wake him up to walk her next door, but she would deal with that later.

"What are you doing here? Isn't this your day off?" Jane asked inquisitively when Emma walked into Morning Glory.

"It is, but I have some work I need to do on the computer. I'll get more accomplished in my office than I will at home." She hoped the questions would stop there.

"I won't bother you, then." Jane smiled.

"Thanks, Jane," she replied as she headed back to her office.

Closing the door behind her, she settled in at her desk. Her stomach flipped nervously. She felt awful about invading Liam's privacy, but she didn't see any other way to find out what she needed to know. She prayed she didn't find anything horrible, because she didn't want to deal with the ramifications.

She performed a quick Google search for *"Liam O'Reilly"* and came up with ten pages of results. She was sure not all of them pertained to her Liam, so she decided to narrow it down a bit by typing *"Liam O'Reilly, Chicago."* That cut the search results in half.

She began clicking on results. There were a few articles about Liam's stellar FBI career. She discovered that he had won several awards, and he'd been recognized many times by the Bureau. He was quite accomplished, and she felt a surge of pride for the man she loved.

She continued clicking through results, perusing page after page of news articles. Nothing at all seemed out of place. There was nothing even remotely related to negative activity involving Liam.

She felt ashamed of herself. She was the worst girlfriend

ever. She should be kicking herself for prying into Liam's past. He was a good man.

Emma was about to close out of the search results when something caught her eye—*"FBI Agent Nearly Catches Jewel Thieves"* jumped off the last page of search results. Curiosity got the better of her, and she continued to read. Her hands began to shake, her head started to spin, and she thought she might pass out. She read the article through once more just to be certain.

A quick glance at the date confirmed the article had been written six years before. It told the story of an FBI agent named Liam O'Reilly who was investigating the case of a jewel thief. What made the case unique was that the primary thief was a woman. She'd been stealing for years and had embezzled close to a billion dollars' worth of jewelry over the course of her career.

The woman's name was Veronica Smith.

The article went on to say that Veronica Smith had a male partner, and that the FBI agent in charge of investigating the case, Liam O'Reilly, had been extremely close to catching them. Supposedly O'Reilly had all the proof he needed and had been waiting in Canada to apprehend them when their plane had crashed.

With the primary suspects dead, he'd been unable to close the case. There was a quote from Liam that stated, *"I will not rest until this case is solved. It might take me years to find the answers, but you can rest assured that I will."*

Emma slowly closed her laptop. She couldn't quite believe what she'd read, and she worked to piece it all together in her mind. Liam had been investigating Veronica, who was a jewel thief. Jacob had been her partner, in more ways than one. Emma's husband had been a criminal, and Liam knew it long before she met him.

He knew the details of her entire life. He understood

more about it than she did, and he had known everything from the beginning. When he'd asked her to share her life story, and she'd so willingly spilled it all out, he had already known.

Once again, she had been betrayed by a man she'd trusted. She had fallen for the deception like a fool. She must be the world's biggest idiot. Liam didn't love her. He'd only gotten close to her in an attempt to learn more about Jacob. He wasn't interested in her; he was investigating her connection to his case.

With Jacob and Veronica dead, she was his only hope of finding information. After all these years, he was still trying to solve the mystery. He had said in the article that he wouldn't give up, and he'd used her to learn more about Jacob.

In a matter of seconds, all the events of the past couple of months raced through her head: Liam buying Veronica's house, Liam coming into Morning Glory and trying to get close to her, Liam making her fall in love with him. The lies and deception were just too much, and she had fallen for all of it.

Emma's stomach churned, and she thought she might be sick. She felt more betrayed by Liam than she had when she found out about Jacob's affair with Veronica. Learning her husband was a jewel thief and led a double life wasn't as hard to swallow as Liam's deception.

What made the discovery so gut-wrenching was that Emma truly loved Liam. It hurt more because she'd given him her whole heart, hadn't held anything back. She'd shown him her fears and vulnerabilities, and she'd trusted him completely. Liam had been lying from the moment she'd first met him. He'd been dishonest with Emma, and worse, dishonest with her girls. That was unforgivable.

She sat in her office for over an hour trying to figure out

what she should do. One thing was certain—Liam had to go. She couldn't stand the thought of seeing him, but he was living in her house. She had to face him long enough to kick him out.

The thought of telling the girls the truth tore her up inside, so she decided she would make something up until she figured out the best way to reveal what happened. They would be devastated when they realized Liam would no longer be a part of their lives, but it couldn't be helped. She had to take action immediately.

Before she could change her mind, she ran home and opened the front door. Her hands trembled and she felt faint, as if she might pass out, but she told herself to be strong. She saw Liam sitting at the kitchen counter working on his laptop. He stood to greet her as she entered the kitchen. It took only a glance for him to realize something happened.

"Emma, what's wrong?" Liam reached out to take her hand.

She pulled her hand away as quickly as if she'd placed it on a hot burner. "Don't even think about touching me. How could you?"

Emma heard the trembling in her voice. She was on the verge of tears, but she wouldn't break down in front of him. She'd shown him enough weakness already.

"Baby, what are you talking about? What happened?" Liam's face was filled with genuine confusion.

"You lied to me from the beginning. Was it all some kind of joke to you? Was it a game to see how quickly I would fall for you? Did you enjoy the show?" Her voice rose in anger. She could feel herself slipping over the edge of reason, but she couldn't stop.

"I don't understand. I don't know what you're talking about."

"Is that so? Does the name Veronica Smith ring a bell?

Because I'm pretty sure you knew her before you knew me. That explains why you're living in her house," she screamed.

Liam's face dropped and she knew he understood. There was no denying it, and to his credit, he didn't even try.

"Emma, please listen to me. It's all true, but you have to believe that I love you," he pleaded.

"Love me? Really? That's your definition of love? Dishonesty and lies? I had that with Jacob! I don't want that kind of love." Emma's words were as sharp as knives as she flung them at him.

"Can I please just explain? When I first came to Beckland, I believed you might know something that could shed some light on the case. But once I got to know you, nothing else mattered. I love you, Emma. I love you, and that has nothing to do with the investigation. I should have told you about my connection to Jacob and Veronica from the start, but I was afraid you wouldn't give me a chance."

"A chance? That's exactly what I gave you! I told you I didn't trust anyone. I told you how hurt I had been, and yet you just continued on, luring me in, making me love you—" Emma's voice broke and her body shook with sobs that she could no longer hold inside. She felt as if her heart was literally breaking inside of her chest. It hurt worse than anything she could imagine.

At the sight of her tears, Liam tried to put his arms around her. She quickly moved away.

"Do. Not. Touch. Me. You have lost that privilege. Get your things and get out of my house. I never want to see you again." Emma spoke through clenched teeth.

"Emma, you don't mean that. You're just angry. I can't leave you here alone. You might be in danger."

"I'll take my chances with the danger. At least I know what to expect. You have five minutes to get your things and get out of my house," she said coldly.

Liam's face drained of all color, but then he trudged upstairs and gathered his belongings. A few minutes later, he grabbed his laptop from the kitchen and carried everything to the front door.

"Emma, please listen to me," he tried again. "I love you."

"I'm through listening to you. Goodbye, Liam." She didn't even glance his way.

"Emma," he pleaded.

"Go!"

Emma heard the front door close as he left. The minute it shut, she ran upstairs and threw herself onto her bed. The room still smelled of Liam's cologne; the scent was so intense that she could almost feel him next to her. She had no idea how she was going to get over the devastation of losing him. It felt like the life had been sucked right out of her. She placed her head on the pillow where Liam had slept and cried herself to sleep.

TWENTY-FIVE

Emma woke at two thirty in the afternoon. In only an hour, her daughters would be home, and she had to pull herself together. She couldn't be weak and weepy when they saw her.

She went to the bathroom sink and splashed cold water on her face. A glance in the mirror told the tale of a woman who had been pushed far beyond her breaking point. Her eyes were puffy and swollen from crying, and her hair was a mess. She dotted some concealer under her eyes and ran a brush through her hair. Hopefully the girls wouldn't notice that their mother was coming apart at the seams.

She felt empty inside. For weeks, she'd been gliding around on a cloud of happiness, and she'd suddenly been dropped back to earth. She'd envisioned her future with Liam in it, and now it just looked bleak. If it weren't for her daughters, she would curl up in a ball and sleep for the next week. But mothers didn't have the option of checking out, so she had to stay strong.

Her children were the driving force that kept her going, and she had to be tough for them. They would be confused about Liam's absence, so she was going to tell them he had to supervise the work on his house. They wouldn't question that.

Emma busied herself with cleaning the house and doing some laundry. She just had to keep moving. That was the only way she would get through it.

At the usual time, she headed outside to meet the bus. The girls sprinted to greet her.

"Hi, Mom. Are you all right?" Lily eyed her mother curiously. She was a discerning child, and if anyone was going to see through the act, it would be her.

"Of course I'm all right." Emma plastered a smile on her face and feigned a happiness she didn't feel.

She hugged her girls tightly and told herself that she only had to play the game until they were in bed. After that, she would allow herself to crumble. She could do anything for a few hours. Dinner preparation was beyond her abilities, though, so she ordered a pizza.

They continued their afternoon, and she thought she was off the hook for explaining Liam's absence. That was wishful thinking.

"Mama, where's Liam? Why isn't he here?" Rose questioned.

"Well, he has some repairs that need to be finished at his house, and he wants to be there to oversee them, so he won't be around for a while." Emma made sure she kept her back turned to them as she spoke. She was a horrible liar, and they would see right through it.

"Is something wrong, Mommy?" Dahlia asked.

"No, honey, it's all good. Liam just has some things to take care of right now." She tried to sound nonchalant.

Thankfully the children dropped the matter, which was good because she wasn't up to discussing Liam any more than she absolutely had to. The best thing would be to not think of him at all, but that was impossible. The truth was, even though she was angry and hurt, she loved him. That was something she'd never get over.

Somehow she made it through the rest of the afternoon and evening. They ate dinner, finished homework, and she performed the girls' entire bedtime routine without breaking down. She even managed to read Rose's favorite bedtime story before kissing them all good night, turning out the lights, and heading back downstairs.

She was just about to turn in for the night when her cell phone rang. With everything that had happened that day, she'd completely forgotten about her stalker. She glanced at the display on the phone, expecting it was the stranger. Instead, her heart dropped when she saw it was Liam.

If she was honest, all she really wanted was to pick up the phone and hear his voice. Her heart practically ached for the sound. She couldn't explain why she still loved him so much after what he'd done, and yet she did. She wished she could forget the whole thing and go back to before she knew the truth.

As her phone continued to ring, she was tempted to do just that, but she didn't. If she couldn't trust Liam, they had no future. He had betrayed her, and he didn't deserve the fierce love she felt for him.

She grabbed her phone and declined the call. With a heavy heart, she trudged upstairs to her room to sleep in a bed that suddenly seemed far too big and empty.

TWENTY-SIX

The following week passed by uneventfully. Liam phoned every day, but each time, she declined the call. She refused to speak with him, knowing if she heard his voice her resolve would crumble and she would run right back to him. She would not be weak. He had lied and used her for information. She would not forgive him, so there was no reason to talk to him

Knowing that didn't make her heart hurt any less, though. She trudged through each day feeling like a zombie. She had no energy, and she felt physically ill. Even though the girls didn't ask, she saw the way they looked at her. They were smart, and they knew something was very wrong.

She hadn't felt that empty when Jacob died; not even the deaths of her parents had sent her into such a downward spiral. The only reason she kept putting one foot in front of the other was because of the girls. She still had to get out of bed each day and care for them, and she still had to operate a business. The only time she gave into the sadness was when she was alone.

If anything positive had come from her misery, it was that

the stranger hadn't called once since Liam had been gone. She'd breathed a sigh of relief that she didn't have to deal with that anymore, thankful he had moved on to other things.

The only bright spot on the horizon was that Sadie would be home that afternoon. She'd been gone a little more than two weeks, and Emma missed her terribly, although she wasn't looking forward to telling her the sad news about Liam. She knew without a doubt that Sadie would stand by her as she had always done, but it wasn't going to be easy to relive the trauma.

Emma drained the pasta she was preparing for dinner. She heard a key jiggle in the lock, and the front door opened. Sadie came inside and the girls excitedly greeted her. They had missed her too.

Emma and Sadie had spoken several times during her vacation, but they'd always kept the conversation casual. Emma hadn't brought up the subject of Liam at all. It was just easier that way. She wanted Sadie to enjoy her visit with her parents, not worry about the train wreck that was happening back in Beckland. When Sadie left for her trip, Emma had been on top of the world. Now it seemed as if life itself had crashed upon her, and it took Sadie only a matter of seconds to recognize that something was wrong.

Emma knew she wasn't looking her best. The situation had taken its toll on her physically, and she had a hard time hiding the dark circles under her eyes. She had barely eaten anything in a week, because she had no appetite. She felt nauseated most days, and she'd even vomited several times from the stress. The girls hadn't asked questions about the changes in her demeanor, though maybe they were perceptive enough to know she didn't want to talk about it. But Sadie knew, and from the expression on her face, she wanted to discuss it at length.

"Hey, munchkins. I have presents for you. Why don't you open them in the living room while I catch up with your mom?" Sadie handed them each a bag filled with gifts.

"Thanks, Aunt Sadie," the girls answered excitedly as they headed into the other room.

Sadie grabbed Emma's hand, led her into the kitchen, and closed the door behind them for privacy. True to form, she didn't begin by asking questions. Instead, she pulled Emma into her arms and held her tightly. That was all it took for the waterworks to begin, Emma dissolving into Sadie's arms as her body shook with sobs. The women had been through so much together that there were times when they didn't need words.

Once the tears ran dry, Emma collapsed at the kitchen table to try to find the words to explain.

"Em, I'm going to check on the girls. I don't want them to come in here and see you like this. I'll be right back, and then I want to know what happened."

Emma was grateful that Sadie was taking charge. That was exactly what she needed.

When Sadie walked back into the kitchen, she sat down at the table and took Emma's hand in hers. She knew she would feel some relief once she confided in her friend. Sadie had seen her through far too many horrible situations, and Emma knew this one would be no different.

"Em, I don't know what's happened, but it must be something with Liam. I've seen you down before, but I've never seen you like this. I'm worried about you. You look like you've been through hell and back. How can I help you?" Sadie squeezed her hand.

Emma spilled the entire story to Sadie. She told her how much she loved Liam, and how they had started talking about a future together. Then she recounted the part about the stalker, and how Liam had moved in to protect them.

Finally she managed to share the discovery of Liam's connection to Veronica and Jacob, and how he had just been using her to solve his case.

Sadie was as shocked as Emma had been to learn that Jacob was a jewel thief. It was a lot to take in, but she listened patiently to her friend's story. Once Emma finished, Sadie sat there quietly, processing it all. Emma saw that she was carefully weighing her words before she spoke.

"Sweetie, I know you feel like Liam betrayed you. I'll admit that he could have handled things differently. But here's where our opinions differ—I don't believe for a second that he doesn't love you. I've seen the two of you together, and that man loves you. He loves your girls. You won't convince me of anything else." Sadie's words were spoken in love, and that was the way Emma took them.

"You may be right, but he still lied to me. Nothing is more important than the truth. If I can't trust him, then I can't be with him," Emma replied stubbornly.

"You aren't in any position to hear me right now, and I get it. You're hurt, and rightfully so. But no matter what he did, Liam loves you. I'm as sure of that as I've ever been about anything." Sadie squeezed Emma's hand tightly.

Emma didn't respond. She couldn't allow herself to open her heart toward Liam even a little. He'd lied to her, and he'd used her. She continued repeating the mantra in her head, certain she would believe it if she said it enough. If you loved someone, you didn't lie to them. That was one thing she was sure of, and she wouldn't forgive Liam. That was the end of the story.

"I have an idea." Sadie released Emma's hand. "I know you've been holding it together in front of the girls, but what you really need is some time alone to fall apart. You need to work it out in your head. I've missed them terribly, and I would love some time with them. What if I take the girls and the pasta upstairs to my place and we can have dinner and a sleepover? That way you can get some sleep and decompress."

"You are truly the best friend I could ask for. That's exactly what I need. I'm miserable, and it'll be nice to wallow in self-pity for a night without having to put on a happy face for the girls," Emma replied as her eyes filled with fresh tears.

Without another word, Sadie instructed the girls to pack an overnight bag. She didn't have to tell them twice; they were excited, to say the least. Emma placed the pasta in a container, handed it to Sadie, hugged them all tightly, and shut the front door behind her.

Then she was alone. The quietness of the house settled around her, but for once she didn't mind. She didn't have to pretend to be anything for anyone at that moment—she could just be broken. She was exhausted, and although it was still early afternoon, she wanted nothing more than to crawl into bed and sleep the night away.

She opted to slip into her nightgown and lie in bed. She could cry, she could sleep, or she could allow herself to be angry. She could do anything she wanted to do.

The problem was, the only thing she wanted to do was call Liam.

Needing a distraction, she flipped on the television and mindlessly surfed the channels for several minutes. Nothing caught her attention, so she settled on a random channel for background noise. She missed Liam desperately, and she was suffering both emotionally and physically. Her body felt as if she'd been run over by a truck. She hadn't known it was possible to love a man that much. She'd been a perfectly functioning woman before he'd come along, and he'd broken her.

She replayed everything over again in her mind. A part of her thought she might have been hasty to break things off with him. Perhaps she should have listened to his side of the story, allowed him to explain. But even as the thoughts ran through her head, she knew there was no explanation good enough for what he'd done. She had no choice but to stand firm. She couldn't forgive him.

Emma knew she needed to sleep, so she settled her head on the fluffy pillow and pulled the blankets up to her chin. She listened as the television droned on in the distance, but her eyes soon grew heavy. Instead of fighting it, she gave in to blissful sleep.

TWENTY-SEVEN

Opening her eyes, she blinked quickly to adjust to the darkened bedroom. She stole a glance at the clock on her nightstand and saw it was 9:30 p.m. She'd already slept for a couple of hours, but she was still exhausted.

She rolled over and whispered a prayer of thanks that Sadie had taken the girls with her for the night. She'd needed a night off more than she'd realized. With only herself to consider, she could take advantage of the empty house and catch up on some much-needed sleep.

Deciding she was finished with the white noise of the television, she grabbed the remote control and turned it off, then snuggled more deeply under her blankets.

Just as she was about to doze off once more, she opened her eyes, thinking she heard a noise downstairs. The quietness of the house settled around her once more. She continued to listen for the strange sound, but heard nothing. She came to the conclusion that it was just the settling of her old house, so she went back to sleep.

TWENTY-EIGHT

EMMA'S EYES FLEW OPEN AS A LARGE HAND COVERED HER mouth. She was so stunned that she couldn't move. She blinked several times, certain she must be dreaming, then wiggled in her bed in an effort to jar herself from what was obviously a nightmare. As her eyes attempted to adjust to the blackness of the room, she managed to turn her head just enough to look at the clock and noticed it was three in the morning. Her brain caught up to what was happening, and she realized it was not a dream.

She tried not to panic, but it was impossible. It was too dark to see anything, and a stranger's hand covered her mouth. She struggled against it and tried to scream, but doing so was useless. The large body leaned on her to the extent that she couldn't move. Terror overtook all rational thought. She had no idea what was going on, but she was clearly in grave danger.

"We meet at last, Emma." As his voice seeped into the quietness of the room, a deep sense of panic set in.

She would know that voice anywhere. It was the stalker, and he was a dangerous man. He hadn't given up on her as she'd assumed with such naiveté. He had simply lulled her into a false sense of security in an effort to catch her completely by surprise. It had been more than a week since she'd received a phone call, and she'd let down her guard. She couldn't even remember if she'd locked her front door before climbing into bed. She berated herself for her carelessness.

Emma forced herself to be calm and began a stream of inner dialogue. She knew that the more she struggled against the man, the more it would bait him. The end result would be deadly. She had to remain level-headed if she wanted to survive.

Her heart raced wildly inside of her chest, and his hand over her mouth made breath control difficult. She forced her breathing to become slow and steady, so as not to hyperventilate. She willed her body to remain still and vowed that she wouldn't scream, no matter how badly she wanted to do so.

"I'm having difficulty seeing your pretty face in the dark, Emma," the man said. "So here's what I'm going to do. I'll turn on the light, but that means I have to take my hand off your mouth. It would be in your best interest not to scream."

Emma nodded slowly to acknowledge that she understood. She would not scream. She would do exactly as he said. Cooperating with the madman was her only hope of making it out of the situation alive.

She closed her eyes and pictured her daughters. She would do whatever she needed to do in order to see them again.

The man turned on the bedside lamp and she caught a glimpse of him for the first time. Although she hadn't given any prior thought to his appearance, when she saw him, she had to admit that he wasn't the type of man whom anyone would label a derelict. In fact, his image would suggest the opposite. He was tall and muscular, well dressed, and quite handsome. She had the fleeting thought that if she'd seen him in her coffee shop, she would have been attracted to him. He had an air about him that suggested a sense of charisma, and she imagined that a great many women were drawn to him. In fact, he probably had women throwing themselves at him.

He wore a charcoal-gray leather jacket and black driving gloves, which she realized were more than likely intended to prevent the leaving of fingerprints. The thought of forensics made her panic all over again. She reconsidered her game plan and decided that she shouldn't cooperate with him after all. Instead, she ought to fight back. She had no idea what he might ask her to do, and complying with his requests could be dangerous. Escaping was the better plan.

He reached into his black bag to look for something and turned his back to her. Making the split-second decision that she needed to get away, she mustered all her courage and leaped off the bed, sprinting toward the open bedroom door. Emma knew that if she could only get out of the bedroom, she could hide somewhere else in the house.

She made it almost halfway across the floor before he turned around. His reflexes were quick and catlike, and it took him only a split second to reach her. The angry look on his handsome face let her know that she'd made the wrong choice. The ferocity of his gaze convinced her that the man could kill her and not think twice about it.

He grabbed her by the hair and threw her onto the bed. Without warning, he slapped her across the face with such force that her head snapped back. She felt the trickle of blood trace down her chin and knew her lip was cut. The blood continued to flow, and she grabbed the sheet to staunch the stream. He glowered at her, his large frame looming above her. She thought for sure that he was going to hit her again, so she braced her body for the impact.

"That was a mistake that you won't want to make again. I didn't come here to hurt you, but you will not leave. I've put a lot of time and effort into you, and we'll know each other very well before the night is over. One way or another, you will tell me what you know." His voice was emotionless and as cold as ice.

He leaned down until his face was only an inch away from Emma's. She had no idea what he would do to her next, and her body trembled with fear. Her lip was still bleeding; she could taste the saltiness as it trickled into her mouth.

"I should introduce myself. My name is Xavier."

Without warning, he closed the gap between them and kissed her roughly, licking the blood that trailed from her lips.

TWENTY-NINE

HE CONTINUED TO KISS HER, AND SHE SWALLOWED HER GAG reflex. She tried to go to another place in her head, but her mind reeled with the realization of his intentions. He grabbed her hair forcefully and tilted her head back so he could look at her. His free hand trailed down her neck and came to rest on the shoulder of her thin nightgown. He grabbed the worn fabric and pulled it so hard that it ripped, fully exposing her body. Her intuition screamed that she was about to be irrevocably violated. Her lip continued to bleed, droplets of red dripping onto her chest, but she knew better than to move. Instead, she forced herself to remain frozen in place.

"You're a lovely woman," Xavier said softly. "All you have to do is cooperate with me. I want to get to know you, Emma. I have so enjoyed our phone calls."

Fear crept up inside of her as his haunting voice echoed in the quiet room. Each word was like a nail being hammered into her coffin.

"Unfortunately I've been told that I have a very bad

temper. I don't like it when my rules aren't followed. I try to control my anger, but I just can't."

As he continued to talk, she came to a decision. She'd learned her lesson. She would follow whatever rules that he had. She would do anything if it meant that she would make it out alive.

"Here's what we're going to do. I need a way to contain you. I can't take the chance of you running off again." Xavier's piercing gray eyes never left hers.

"I won't run." Emma's voice trembled.

"I don't believe you." Xavier laughed, and when he did, his face changed. He didn't seem quite so threatening. But the moment was fleeting, and the cold look returned to his eyes nearly as quickly as it had gone. "We're going to go downstairs."

Xavier gripped her hair tightly so she couldn't move her head, then released it and grabbed both of her arms, pulling her roughly to a standing position. The remnants of her nightgown fluttered to the floor. When Xavier eyed her body hungrily, she knew what was about to happen. She had to distract him. She could not allow him to violate her in that way, as she might never recover.

"Xavier, I'm cold. Can I please have my robe? I'll do whatever you want, but let me cover up," she pleaded with him, hoping to reach some part of him that was still human.

"It seems a shame to cover such beauty." Xavier trailed his fingertip across her jaw, down her neck, and rested it on her collarbone. She shuddered at the stark look of desire in his eyes. He rubbed his palms up and down her arms.

"Your skin is so soft. It feels like satin. Liam is a lucky man." Xavier slid his hands over her skin, and although it sickened her, she had no choice but to let him.

"Where is your robe?"

His words surprised her, but she managed to answer,

"It's hanging on the back of the bathroom door. If you'll get it for me, I'll stand right here. I promise I won't run." She was thankful that he was going to allow her to cover herself.

He disappeared briefly into the bathroom and returned with the robe. "I'll bring this downstairs, but I'm not quite ready to let you have it. I want to look at you a while longer."

Xavier threw her robe across his shoulder, then scooped Emma into his huge arms as if she were no larger than a child. Being held by her captor almost tenderly was awkward and terrifying. She was completely at his mercy. Trying not to imagine all the things he might do, she continued telling herself to stay calm and do whatever he asked. She refused to die at the hands of a madman.

He carried her down the hall and expertly maneuvered her down the stairs without turning on a single light. He ambled along, seemingly unhurried. As he held her, he caressed her skin, lowered his head into her hair, and breathed in her scent. He seemed to be enjoying the experience.

"It's a shame that we had to meet under such circumstances, Emma. But it won't be long before you develop feelings for me. Discovering my feelings for you has been a pleasant surprise." He continued slowly toward the kitchen.

Her body trembled in fear, and she fought to keep the terror at bay. She knew exactly what he intended to do to her, and although she knew she couldn't let it happen, she had no idea how to prevent it. She was already naked, and he was in control. He was much stronger than she was, and there was no doubt that he could overpower her if it came to that. He had the ability to do anything he wanted. All she could do was distract him and keep him talking.

"I'm still confused. I don't know what you want from me." Somehow she managed to control her voice and keep it calm and steady. "I will tell you whatever you want to know, but I have no idea what that is."

"You know exactly what I want. You're just playing me for a fool and pretending you don't know what I'm looking for. Women are all the same. They lure you in with their beauty and then play games with your mind."

Emma saw they had reached the kitchen. Xavier looked around as if trying to decide what he should do next. He bent down and instructed her to stand. Her back was against his chest and his arms remained wrapped around her body, his soft leather jacket next her skin. If someone were to view the scene as an outsider, it might appear that the two were lovers. He held her almost tenderly as his hands roamed over her body. She willed herself to remain still even though her stomach lurched in disgust.

Breaking away, he walked to the kitchen table, pulled a chair out from under the table, and commanded her to sit on it. Then he dropped to his knees and knelt before her, reached into his pocket, and pulled out a pair of zip ties.

"If you remain still, these won't hurt you. Your skin is so beautiful, and I wouldn't want to mark it unnecessarily." Xavier kissed her arms and wrists.

He observed her face and frowned when his eyes rested on her cut lip, almost like he was sorry he'd hit her. He reached out and touched the wound carefully as he brought his face to hers and kissed her once more. She had resolved to let him do whatever he wanted, as long as he let her live, though she was confused by his actions. He vacillated between intense anger and tender, loving caresses. There was no question that he was volatile and unstable. She knew she should tread lightly.

He placed her hands behind her and zip-tied one wrist to each back post of the chair, then did the same with her legs. She was trapped. Once he was certain that she couldn't move, he walked across the room and turned on the light above the sink. It didn't illuminate the entire room, but it did allow her to see his face more clearly. She had no idea what he would do next.

"I didn't want things to go this way, Emma. You should have just told me where they were from the beginning." Xavier paced the floor. It was obvious that all traces of tenderness were gone. The cold, terrifying look of steel had returned to his eyes.

"I swear I don't know what you mean. If I did, I would tell you. What are you talking about?"

Xavier's face contorted with rage. He towered over her, and she was sure he was going to hit her again.

"The jewels, Emma!" His voice grew louder. "Where are the jewels?"

Understanding hit her like Xavier's slap in the face. Suddenly all the pieces of the puzzle came together. He was somehow connected to the jewels, to Jacob, to Veronica, and to Liam. He thought she was a part of it, and in that moment, she knew the only chance she had of getting out alive was making him believe that she knew where they were. Lying wasn't her strong suit, but her ability to do so was the only thing keeping her alive. Her very existence depended on convincing him that she knew where they were.

"The jewels. Yes, I know all about them." She forced her voice not to tremble. "But how do you know about them?"

"I know about them because they were my idea!" Xavier screamed. "I taught Veronica everything I knew. When she married me, she knew nothing. All she cared about was that I had money and she wanted it. Buried beneath her beauty was a woman who was as cold as ice. The only thing she wanted was to be rich."

She tried to hide her shock at learning Xavier was Veronica's husband. She needed to keep him talking.

"You were married to Veronica? She was my neighbor." She glanced up at Xavier and saw he had gone somewhere else in his head.

"She was so beautiful. I thought she loved me. She pretended to, but the only thing she loved was money. When she found out I was a jewel thief, she begged me to teach her the ropes. She told me she would be good at it because no one would suspect her, and she was right. She was far better at it than I ever was. I only did small-time jobs. It was good money, but it wasn't enough for Veronica. She wanted more, so she hatched this scheme to start hitting up the ultra-rich set. I told her that was too risky, but she wouldn't listen. She said if I wouldn't help her, she'd find someone who would."

Xavier was so lost in the past, that it was almost as if he had forgotten Emma was there. She eyed the room frantically, trying to come up with a plan, but it was no use. She was zip-tied to a chair, completely naked. She had to keep him talking.

"Finding out that she didn't love you must have been painful. It sounds like you loved her very much." She tried her best to sound sympathetic.

"She left me. I came home one day and she was waiting for me at the door with her bags packed. She told me she'd found a new partner, some guy named Jacob. But you already knew that, didn't you?" He glared coldly at her.

"We were both betrayed, Xavier," she said, trying to convince him that they shared a common bond. She needed to keep him on her side.

"Yes, we were. Their partnership worked out pretty well. They managed to steal billions of dollars' worth of jewelry until the FBI got wise to their game. Your boyfriend Liam thought he could catch them. He might have, too, if they hadn't died in that plane crash," Xavier continued. "And I'm willing to bet that you know exactly where those jewels are.

There's no way you were married to that guy and didn't know."

"Do you really think I knew? Think about it, Xavier. What woman would stay with a husband who was sleeping with another woman and stealing jewels with her? You're a smart man. Does that sound logical to you?" Tired of lying, Emma gained courage as she spoke. "I didn't know about Jacob and Veronica. I didn't know they were having an affair, and I certainly didn't know my husband and my neighbor were jewel thieves."

Xavier slapped her again, only much harder. The cut on her lip reopened and began bleeding profusely, the blood running down her chin and dripping onto her chest. He was angrier than he had been before, and he was going to seriously hurt her if she didn't get help. Her plan to remain compliant and agreeable was not going to work.

Xavier had crossed over into a very dark place, and she knew she could no longer reason with him. So she did the only thing she could think of to do—she screamed as loudly as she could.

The house was huge, and the chances of anyone hearing her were slim, but she thought if she could scream loudly enough, Sadie might hear her, at least. When she screamed again, rage contorted his face and he hit her forcefully. It wasn't a slap that time but a punch. As he pummeled her face, he yelled at her to stop. But she didn't listen. She screamed as if her life depended on it, because it did.

Xavier continued punching her, and she felt herself slipping in and out of consciousness. The room was spinning and bile rose in her throat. She closed her eyes and pushed down the need to vomit as she continued to yell.

Suddenly the sound of shattering glass filled the room. Xavier stopped punching her and pivoted quickly, startled by the sound. Running footsteps were followed by a large thud.

She attempted to open her eyes, but she couldn't see clearly. She just managed to make out Xavier's form face-down on the floor, his wrists being handcuffed behind him. The last thing she saw before she lost consciousness was Liam, who had his gun pointed at Xavier's head.

THIRTY

EMMA WOKE UP IN A HOSPITAL ROOM. HER HEAD WAS throbbing, and she could only see out of one eye. She touched her face and felt her right eye, which was puffy and swollen to several times its usual size. She held up her hand, but she couldn't see it. Her lip hurt. She traced her fingertips over it carefully and discovered that she had several stitches.

She had no idea how long she'd been out, and it seemed like she was alone in the room. She tried to sit up, but she couldn't. There wasn't an inch of her body that wasn't in excruciating pain. She looked out of the corner of her good eye and noticed Liam was asleep in a chair across the room.

She tried very hard to remember the events that occurred before she passed out. She recalled the sound of shattering glass, guessing it had been the window breaking as Liam sailed through it. He had taken Xavier down and handcuffed him, and she remembered that Liam had pointed his gun at the man and screamed at him to stay still. She struggled to remember more, but she couldn't. It was a complete blank. She had no idea what day it was or how long she'd been in the hospital. She didn't know if her girls were safe, but she knew they must be worried sick about her.

"Liam." She hoped he would hear her and wake up.

His eyes fluttered open and he sat up quickly. Rushing to her side, he reached out and grabbed her hand.

"Emma, you're awake," he said with a wide smile. "How are you feeling?"

"Probably about as good as I look." She attempted a smile, then winced in pain because of the stitches in her lip. "How long have I been here?"

"Since yesterday." Liam pulled a chair next to the bed and sat down. "Do you remember what happened?"

She told him what she remembered up to the point where she passed out. Then she asked about the girls. He assured her that they were fine, and he began to fill in some of the blanks for her. Sadie had run downstairs when she heard the commotion. She found Liam standing over Xavier, and he'd instructed her to call 911. Thankfully the girls had been asleep, and Sadie told them a watered-down version of the story the next morning. They were staying with her, and she would bring them by after school.

"Everything makes sense except for one thing. Why were you at my house? Don't get me wrong, I'm glad you were there, but how did you know I was in trouble?" She found it hard to look in Liam's eyes after everything that had happened between them.

"Emma, I know you don't believe me, but I love you. I told you I would protect you, and I meant it. I knew you were in some kind of trouble, so when you kicked me out, I still had to find a way to watch over you. I took the chance that you would be all right during the day, but I parked my car outside of your house every single night. I had to be sure you and the girls were safe."

She stared at him in amazement as she tried to take it all

in. Liam had parked outside of her house every night to watch over them after she had kicked him out. If she was being honest, that didn't sound like a man who had been using her. It didn't sound like a man who was only interested in what she could do for him. Tiny specks of doubt crept in, and she began to question her emotions. Perhaps she'd been wrong about him. Maybe he really did love her.

"When I heard you scream, I knew something was wrong. By the way, you have the loudest scream of anyone I have ever heard." Liam smiled, trying to lighten the tense moment. "I tried the front door, but of course it was locked. I'd left my key at my house, so the only choice was to come in through the window. When I saw what he had done to you, I wanted to kill him. I would have, too, but I knew I needed him alive to question him. You were naked and bleeding and tied to the chair. I hate myself for letting that happen to you."

"Liam, you couldn't have known about this. Xavier was a crazy man. He was completely irrational and unstable. He thought I knew where the jewels were. That's what he wanted all along. When he realized I didn't know, he became furious. If you hadn't come in when you did, he would have killed me. You saved my life." She reached for his hand.

"Emma, did he…?" Liam wasn't able to bring himself to say the words.

"No, Liam, he didn't." She knew exactly what he was asking, and thankfully the answer was no.

"Thank God. If he had touched you like that, I would go kill him right now. I couldn't stand it. I'm so sorry he hurt you at all. I'm sorry I didn't protect you." The agony on his face was almost more than she could bear.

"Please don't apologize. It's over now," she said as she squeezed his hand. "By the way, what's up with the jewels? Is he crazy, or are they hidden somewhere?"

"Once I had him in custody, I questioned him. He let it

slip that Veronica bragged about hiding a huge stash of jewels behind a false wall of her house. It sounded like the perfect plan. After interrogating him, I went back to my house and found the wall. Sure enough, all of the jewels were inside. They'd been right there the whole time. Finally, after almost seven years, I can say the case is closed. They're sending out a crew today to gather the jewels for evidence. They'll be processed and returned to the people they belong to," Liam explained with a smile.

She was relieved to know that the case of the missing jewels was closed. It was a chapter of her life that she was ready to put behind her. They had been the source of so much pain and trauma in her life, and she was glad they would be returned to their rightful owners.

The only thing left to figure out was whether or not she could forgive Liam. She didn't know how things were going to turn out. He had saved her life, and she knew she still loved him. No matter what had happened or how it had come to be, she loved him. She was angry at him, but that didn't seem to matter as much in light of what she'd experienced.

She had almost died, and she'd been given a second chance. She shouldn't waste that chance by being angry over something she couldn't change. The circumstances that had brought them together were not ideal, but the fact remained that she loved him, and she knew in her heart that he loved her too. Maybe he had been dishonest about his connection to Jacob, and that might take some time to get over, but thanks to Liam, time was something that she had.

She was trying to figure out how to put her feelings into words when the door of the hospital room opened. A woman whom Emma assumed was her doctor walked in.

"Glad to see you're awake, Emma. You gave us a bit of a scare," said the woman whose nametag read Dr. Woods.

"Thank you. I'm glad to be awake too."

"I need to do an exam. Your blood test showed something we need to talk about. Could you please excuse us, Mr. O'Reilly?" Dr. Woods said kindly.

"Do you want me to stay, Emma?" Liam's face registered concern.

"I'll be fine. Can you please call Sadie and tell her I'm awake and can't wait to see her and the girls?" She squeezed his hand. She was nervous about the exam, and she didn't want Liam there for it.

He kissed her forehead lightly before he left the room.

"Are you feeling okay? I know you're in pain because of your injuries. You were beaten quite badly," Dr. Woods said as she placed a blood pressure cuff on Emma's arm.

"I'm sore. I've been feeling out of sorts lately, even before the incident. I've been tired and nauseated, but I've also been under a lot of stress." She didn't want to go into the details of her personal life, but she hoped Dr. Woods could shed some light on why she'd been feeling so sick. "Of course, right now I just feel like I was run over by a truck."

"Your blood tests show you're severely anemic, Emma. That could account for your fatigue," Dr. Woods answered.

"Anemic? That's bad, right? But I can just take something for it, can't I?"

"I'm actually more concerned about the anemia than I am with the injuries from your attack. You'll heal quickly, believe it or not. You didn't suffer any broken bones. You may want to consider talking with someone, though. An attack like what you suffered can cause mental trauma long after the physical wounds heal. Which brings me back to the anemia. In your condition, it's important that you get a good iron supplement immediately," Dr. Woods continued as she wrote something on the chart.

"My condition?" Emma didn't understand.

"It's a miracle really, considering what you've endured. We were amazed that there was no damage done to the baby. After they brought you in, we did a blood test and realized you were pregnant. We did an ultrasound to check out the baby, and everything looks just fine."

"Baby? I think there must be a mistake. I'm not pregnant," Emma stammered.

"Yes you are. There's no question about it. You're pregnant." Dr. Woods smiled.

Emma was stunned. She was pregnant with Liam's child. They were going to have a baby. She didn't know how it had gotten past her. How had she not known? Suddenly it all made sense—the nausea, the tiredness, the lethargy. She'd thought it was just because of stress.

She immediately wondered how Liam would take the news.

Dr. Woods finished writing on the chart and told Liam he could come back inside. He sat down next to Emma on the bed.

"Is everything okay? What did Dr. Woods mean about something they found in the blood test?" He was obviously concerned.

"I'm anemic. She wanted to prescribe an iron supplement."

"Anemia can be bad, Emma. Are you going to be all right?" Liam gripped her hand tightly.

She took a deep breath. It was now or never. "I think it should clear up in about nine months or so."

"Nine months?" Liam asked. "That's awfully specific."

"Yeah, my anemia will probably clear up about the time I have the baby. It's a pretty common thing during pregnancy." She swallowed hard as her eyes filled with tears.

"Emma, you're pregnant?" Liam gazed at her in amazement. "How long have you known?"

"About four minutes now. That's what the doctor just told me. I had no idea. I can't believe I didn't piece it together with the way I've been feeling. I just thought it was stress," she laughed.

"We're going to have a baby. We're going to be a family—you, me, the girls, and our baby." Liam's excitement was obvious.

Suddenly he stopped and his face fell. "I'm sorry. I got carried away. I know you don't trust me, and I respect that. I won't push you to change your mind. But I do love you, Emma. I love you with all my heart. I'm so sorry that I wasn't honest with you from the beginning. That is the biggest regret of my life."

Her feelings were playing tug-of-war inside of her. She was happy, scared, excited, nervous, and confused all at the same time. If she could get past the feelings of hurt and betrayal, she knew she wanted nothing more than to be a family with Liam. They had created a new life together. It wasn't something they'd planned, but it was exactly what she wanted.

Looking at Liam, she knew her feelings were solid, and what they felt for one another was true. It was the real deal. It didn't come along every day, and she needed to grab it and hold onto it.

"I love you, Liam," she said simply.

Slowly dropping to one knee, he took her hand in his, reached into his pocket, and pulled out a ring. She gasped.

"Emma, this was my grandmother's ring. I loved her very much. She gave this to me before she died and told me to make sure the woman I chose to give it to was worthy of my love. I've been carrying it around with me for days, hoping I could convince you to change your mind and listen to me. I know I came into your life under false pretenses, and I'm not proud of that, but I promise you that no man could ever love you more. I want to love and protect you for the rest of my life. I want you, me, the girls, and our baby to be a family." Liam's voice shook with emotion. "Will you be my wife?"

He was everything she'd ever wanted, and she couldn't imagine spending her life any other way than with him.

"Yes, Liam, I'll marry you." Tears spilled down her cheeks.

Liam slipped the ring onto her finger. It was a perfect fit, a beautiful square-cut center stone in an antique setting. The facets of the diamond sparkled in the light.

She looked into the eyes of the man she loved. They may not have been brought together under the best of circumstances, but that didn't matter anymore. What mattered was that in a crazy, hectic, mixed-up world, they'd found one another.

Liam had come to her during the investigation of her husband, trying to get to the bottom of a case that he was desperate to solve, but for Emma, Liam had solved a bigger problem. He'd broken down her walls and shown her she could love again. He'd replaced her fear with courage. He'd caused her to investigate her own heart, a heart that had been filled with barriers, broken by hurt and betrayal. He had taken her shattered heart and mended it with his love and patience. He had brought her back to life, and whatever the future held, they would face it together.

THIS STORY CONTINUES **in *For Better or For Worse* (The Vows Book 2).**

THANKS

Thanks for reading *To Have and To Hold* (The Vows Trilogy Book 1). I do hope you enjoyed Emma's story. I appreciate your help in spreading the word, including telling a friend. Before you go, it would mean so much to me if you would take a few minutes to write a review and share how you feel about my story so others may find my work. Reviews really do help readers find books. Please leave a review on your favorite book site.

Don't miss out on New Releases, Exclusive Giveaways and much more!

Join my newsletter: http://eepurl.com/cfhMXf
Like me on Facebook: www.facebook.com/heidireneemason
Join my reader group: Heidi's Tribe:
https://www.facebook.com/groups/346156819065335
Follow me on Twitter: @heidireneemason
Follow me on Instagram: @author_heidireneemason
Follow me on BookBub:
https://www.bookbub.com/authors/heidi-renee-mason

Visit my website for my current booklist:
www.heidireneemason.com

I'd love to hear from you directly, too. Please feel free to email me at: heidisbooks999@gmail.com or check out my website www.heidireneemason.com for updates.

ABOUT THE PUBLISHER

Hot Tree Publishing opened its doors in 2015 with an aspiration to bring quality fiction to the world of readers. With the initial focus on romance and a wide spread of romance subgenres, Hot Tree Publishing have since opened their first imprint, Tangled Tree Publishing, specializing in crime, mystery, suspense, and thriller.

Firmly seated in the industry as a leading editing provider to independent authors and small publishing houses, Hot Tree Publishing is the sister company to Hot Tree Editing, founded in 2012. Having established in-house editing and promotions, plus having a well-respected market presence, Hot Tree Publishing endeavors to be a leader in bringing quality stories to the world of readers.

Interested in discovering more amazing reads brought to you by Hot Tree Publishing? Head over to the website for information:

www.hottreepublishing.com